SUPER
FREAK

Also by Brian Falkner

Henry and the Flea
The Real Thing

SUPER FREAK

Brian Falkner

MALLINSON RENDEL

First published in 2005 by
Mallinson Rendel Publishers Limited
PO Box 9409, Wellington, New Zealand
www.mallinsonrendel.co.nz

Reprinted 2006

© Brian Falkner 2005
www.brianfalkner.co.nz

ISBN 0-908783-98-1
ISBN 978-0-908783-98-4

National Library of New Zealand Cataloguing-in-Publication Data

Falkner, Brian.
Super freak / by Brian Falkner.
[1. Psychic ability—Fiction. 2. Bullying—Fiction. 3. Schools—Fiction.]
I. Title.
NZ823.3—dc 22

Cover design Vida Kelly
Typesetting by Hamish Thompson
Printed in China through Colorcraft Ltd, Hong Kong

Contents

Author's Notes

Once again the names of a number of New Zealand school children appear in this book. These children won competitions I run as part of my talks to schools around the country. Congratulations to: Matthew Clay (Wadestown School), Chelsie Burnett (Waikanae School), Stacey Anderson (Limehills School) and Minet Brits (Paraparaumu Beach School) along with the winners from the 2004 Storylines Festival: Tom Prebble, Jordan Hoffman-Herbert and Nicholas Priddey.

Thanks to Laura Falkner for the haiku in chapter 29.

For Kevin E and Michael M
The boys who ran into the storm

1

Forward - Mind Matters

Where do thoughts come from?

You know, like you're sitting in maths and the teacher is droning on about isosceles triangles, and suddenly into your mind pops the thought that you'd really like a big date scone with jam and whipped cream. Which has nothing to do with isosceles triangles.

Or you're sitting on the bus on the way home from school and all at once you imagine that the bus is going to lift off the ground like a UFO and fly out into orbit.

Where do thoughts like that come from? I don't know. I'm not a scientist, or a psychologist or anything like that. I'm just a kid. But I do know where some thoughts come from. Like the time that Frau Blüchner in French class wrote 'knickers' on the board instead of 'naître'. I know where that thought came from. It came from me.

Perhaps I should explain. Let's start with this: my name is Jacob John Smith, and this is the story of the crime of the century.

2

Words of Wisdom

The English language, I decided, was full of long, wise and wonderful words, which were rarely used, even by teachers. As a full-time native speaker of the language I felt it was my duty to use most of these words as often as possible, and all of them at least once in my life.

So, after four schools in four years, the library and the dictionary were my best friends.

It isn't easy shifting schools. I had started school with a couple of mates from kindy, and was happily ensconced in primary school through the ages of five, six, and part of my third year, when, just after my birthday, my dad's company shifted him from Oamaru to Ashburton.

'He'll make friends easily,' they said; *they* being everyone from my mum and dad, to my new teachers, grandparents and assorted aunts and uncles. Only it wasn't easy. Kevin and Mike, my absolute best mates in Oamaru, came to see me off when we left for Ashburton one Saturday morning in July. They waved, and I waved back and thought about how much I was going to miss them, but I waited until they were well out of sight until I cried. And I kept crying the whole way to

Ashburton, despite my big sister April threatening to thump me, and Mum eventually saying that if I didn't stop it I would miss out on McDonalds for lunch, and Dad saying that if I didn't shut up he was going to leave me on the side of the road.

Even Gumbo, the family dog, lay on the back seat in between April and me and put his front paws over his ears.

April thumped me. I missed out on McDonalds (we had a dry, papery sandwich from a roadside café instead), but I didn't get left on the side of the road. Things might have been different if I had.

They gave me a school-buddy at Allenton Primary in Ashburton. That's a kid who is assigned by the teacher to show you around. I think the idea is to help you get to know people and make friends.

The only problem was my school-buddy was a creep named Alex Kerkoff, and you could have found a worse school-buddy, but it would have taken a lot of trying. I don't know why he was assigned to me. Maybe it was a punishment, or maybe it was just his turn.

The first lunchtime, Alex showed me where the toilets, library, and sick-room were, then disappeared to play some stupid trading card game with his friends. I sat around on a wooden bench for a while, looking at the wintery drizzle and, after a while, I found my way to the library.

At the end of lunch-break, Alex was waiting for me outside the classroom door, and we walked in as though we had spent the whole lunchtime together. As if we were buddies.

I did make friends, though, eventually, Sam and Niwa. Andy too, I suppose, and Christian Jobson, although he was in another class. Not quite close friends, like Kevin and Mike had been, but good mates all the same.

So, you can't imagine how devastated I was when my mum and dad announced to me, not much more than a year after we'd arrived in Ashburton, that he'd been promoted and we were moving to Wellington.

My name is Jacob John Smith, and that's an unfortunate name in some ways. John was my father's name, and Jacob was just a name my parents liked. But there's a kids' song called John Jacob Jingleheimer Smith, and my name was just a little too close to that for comfort.

In my third primary school they used to walk past the library singing it but changing the lyrics to something much ruder.

John Jacob Jingleheimer Smith, his name is your name too.
And you're such a smarty pants,
You're a real farty pants.
Go home John Jacob Jingleheimer Smith.

I said it was rude. I never said it was clever.

The library, which had been my retreat from boredom, became my refuge from their taunts, from their derision. It became my castle.

I didn't make any real friends in Wellington, but I was only there for eighteen months. Dad worked for a nationwide network of radio stations and, when they were bought out by some overseas company, half the staff – including Dad – lost their jobs. So, we shifted again, this time to Auckland. I'm sure I would have made some friends if I had stayed in Wellington a bit longer. I'm quite sure of that. Quite sure.

We shifted over Christmas and I think that helped because, when I started at Glenfield Intermediate, I wasn't the only stranger. The kids were from lots of different primary schools and I didn't have to break into a class mid-year.

I made friends almost immediately with a red-haired firecracker of a boy named Tommy Semper. We got along great. We had the same sense of humour, liked (or didn't like) the same sports, and generally had a good time whenever we were around each other.

Only thing was, he didn't return to school after the first term holidays. This time it wasn't me that was transferred away, it was him. Tommy's father was a representative of a big Italian firm, and he got recalled to Italy. The first I knew was when Mrs Abernethy, our teacher, called out the roll at the start of class on the first day back. I wanted to skip class that day, I felt sick. But I wasn't really sick, and no amount of pleading would convince Mrs Abernethy otherwise. It occurred to me, possibly for the first time, how my life was completely out of my control. People told me what to do. Things happened to me. I had no say in anything. I was just a leaf swept up in a storm.

Andrew Allen transferred into our class during that term, his family had moved up from New Plymouth. For the first couple of weeks he looked as lost and lonely as I was. I didn't try to make friends with him, though. Friends moved away. They hurt you, and it wasn't even their fault. Two long years at Intermediate School and I managed to get though them without making a single friend.

The only thing you could rely on, the one thing that was always there, was the library. And the library was full of books, and the books were full of words. Long, wise and wonderful words.

3

The First Clue

The first time I got a clue was in PE.

Physical Education it stands for, although, personally, I thought Persecution and Excruciation were more appropriate. High School was a big change from Intermediate, in many ways, some for the better and some for the worse. One of the worse was PE. Old Mr Saltham, who had been in the navy, was in charge of the Persecution & Excruciation department, and he took our class for PE.

Mr Saltham, 'Old Sea Salt' we called him, because of his time in the navy, barked orders as though you were deck hands. If you didn't succeed at something he'd make you do it again, and if you simply *couldn't* succeed at something he'd make you keep trying until you'd humiliated yourself in front of the whole class, and then he'd give you detention.

I admit that this approach actually worked on some kids. Some kids who were lacking in confidence would end up succeeding at something they didn't think they could do, and that gave them the confidence to try other things they didn't think they could do and before long they were into everything; so Old Sea Salt did have some success.

However, that was some kids. Not all kids. For many of us, and you'll notice that I said *us,* Saltham's tactics were terrifying and made us even more convinced that we were useless at anything physically demanding.

Old Sea Salt was short and wiry and what little hair he had was cropped close to his scalp. He may not have been all that tall, but he seemed twice the size when he started shouting. I suppose he was used to dealing with a tough bunch of sailors, so kids like us were easy meat.

One of Saltham's favourite exercises was a version of bullrush. It was a bit simpler, though, and much more violent. He'd line up half the class on one side of the gym, and the other half on the other side. In the dead centre of the floor was a big circle which was something to do with netball. When he blew his whistle, everybody had to run to the other side of the hall. But they had to run through the circle. It was like rush hour on one of those Japanese commuter trains where they pack people in like sardines, only half the people were running in one direction, and the rest were going in the other. If you were on the outside you risked getting bumped out of the circle and having to do push-ups. If you were on the inside it was like being crushed in a lemon squeezer.

The last time we had done the exercise I had been on the inside. That was tough, because I was one of the smaller kids in the class and behind me I'd had a couple of the biggest, while in front of me, going the other way, had been the captain of the rugby league team, Phil Domane, and his huge mate (and star league player) Blocker Blüchner. I'd been squeezed between the two sides until I thought I was going to pop up into the air like an orange pip you squeeze between your fingers. I couldn't breathe. I couldn't even get enough air into my lungs to scream, which was probably just as well as they would have thought I was a whooss, and I would have got detention as well.

Just when I'd thought I was dead, the pressure from behind had squeezed me through a small gap between Phil and Blocker and, after taking an anonymous elbow in the side of the head that made my eyes water, and bouncing off a few other guys, I was finally through and over to the other wall.

That had been a week earlier. Now it was PE again, and I was scared out of my wits that we were going to have to go through the same thing. Only this time I might not be so lucky. This time I might not survive.

The lesson was just all the usual tortures until the last few minutes. We had finished a long arduous exercise that involved throwing around medicine balls, and had packed the gear away. Then we just milled around for a moment wondering what Old Sea Salt would set us to do for the last few minutes of the period.

He walked to the centre of the hall, in the middle of the netball circle and looked at us. There were just four minutes left in the period. Saltham never let you go early; it would be undisciplined. I could see him considering, and I knew he was going to make us do the bullrush exercise.

Don't do the bullrush exercise, I thought at him desperately, trying to will him not to. *Let them all go early.* I thought it over and over, staring at him, as if somehow I could make up his mind for him.

'That's enough for today,' he said at last, glancing up at the clock on the wall. 'Off you go, get changed, see you on Thursday.'

Everybody rushed for the changing rooms, surprised beyond belief. But as Old Sea Salt walked past me, staring

straight ahead, I thought he looked a little surprised as well.
I didn't think much of it, though. Just lucky, I thought.
Until the next time.

4

Detention

It was Thursday. The *next time* was still a couple of days away.
It was sunny and warm, after a long wet spell, and some kids
were spinning around on the school fields like puppies chasing
their tails, having too much fun to head off home, even though
school had finished.

Not me though. I was in detention. Again.

Now, I don't want you to get the wrong idea here. I don't
want you to start thinking that I was a bad kid. I mean, sure, I
seemed to spend a lot of time in detention, and I'd been called
into the Principal's office for a stern talking-to on more than
one occasion, and I was ever-grateful that they'd outlawed the
cane many years ago, but it was almost never my fault.

You know how some kids just seem to attract trouble? Well,
I was one of those kids. And I don't care if you believe me or
not.

OK, maybe I did do a few bad things at the beginning, like
the joke with the water-balloon, the roll of toilet-paper, and
Mrs Rossler's handbag, but she'd deserved it anyway for making
fun of me in history. And if I'd been sensible, I'd never have
done what I did with the school's prize-winning totem pole,

but it was really funny and I hadn't thought I'd get caught. And, yes, there were a few unauthorised chemistry experiments involving some talcum powder and the school cat.

But it was all just fun stuff. I was not a bad kid.

I'm not saying I was perfect. I wasn't a genius like Amy Spring, who'd won the national Mathex competition, or a school hero like Blocker Blüchner, the try-scoring front-row forward of the under fifteens school rugby league team.

But I certainly didn't deserve all the crap that seemed to come my way.

So, there I was, sitting in detention, pen in hand, paper in front of me, looking out of the window watching Phil, Emilio and Blocker kick a football around on top field. I lowered my eyes and flashed evil thoughts at Blocker, and he dropped an easy catch, which made the others laugh. Good, I thought. I wouldn't even be in detention if it wasn't for Blocker.

He had chucked a flask of potassium permanganate solution (that purpley stuff) half-way across the science lab to me when the teacher wasn't looking, but I had fumbled and dropped it. It had smashed and gone all over Tom Prebble's schoolbag and, somehow, I had ended up taking the rap.

Of course I had protested my innocence, but he was the star of the league team, and I was a known trouble-maker. So, who were they going to believe?

I turned back to my detention assignment. I had to write an essay on capital punishment in New Zealand, the pros and cons. Capital punishment, if you don't know, is the death penalty for serious crimes like murder.

I wasn't quite sure why they'd chosen that subject for the detention essay. Maybe it was a kind of threat. Maybe they were thinking of introducing it at Glenfield. I decided that I'd better write an essay strongly opposed to capital punishment, just in case.

I looked around the room. There was only one other kid in detention today, Toby Watson. He was staring at his blank refill pad with a panicky expression on his face. I don't know why writing essays terrifies most kids. All you have to do is decide what your opinion is, then express it clearly in nice simple words that even teachers can understand.

I also can't understand why they use essays as a punishment. I really enjoyed writing essays, but it seemed as if the teachers were saying writing was a bad thing, a thing so horrible that you'd only do it as a punishment.

Then they go and complain that it's hard to get kids to write stories and stuff nowadays. Go figure!

Four o'clock came and I had long finished my two page essay. I walked out past Toby, who had only done half a page, and put it on the teacher's desk as I left.

The next day my life changed for ever.

5

The Artificial Kid

What if there was this giant American corporation that made robots? A really secret corporation which made top secret test models for the US Army or the CIA; robots that looked just like human beings. And what if this corporation made a robot like a kid? An artificial schoolkid. And maybe they wanted to see how well the robot would do if it was put in a class of regular kids. To see if the other kids noticed.

I know it sounds a bit far fetched, but what if it were true?

Ben Holly was thirteen years old, he was in my class for French and Science, and I was sure he was a robot.

He was a very good one, no doubt about that. Very well made with highly advanced technology. He looked just like a human, and I don't think any of the other kids at school could tell he was really a robot. They knew there was something a little strange about him and nobody played with him or talked to him much. He was an outsider like me.

But I could tell that he was artificial. I noticed little things about the way he moved and the way he spoke which gave it away. When he walked, or moved his arms, every little movement was exact. Just like a robot. He made one careful, precise movement after another, not like other kids who were usually just a big tangle of arms and legs. If you've ever seen one of those mechanical, robotic arms working on a Japanese car factory assembly line, then you can understand the sort of movements he made.

If you walked behind him and listened really carefully, you could hear the pneumatics that powered his mechanical arms and legs. Sort of a 'sssshhhh'ing sound.

Then, there was the way his eyes moved; that was a dead giveaway. His eyes didn't flick around all over the place like normal kids' eyes. They stayed staring precisely on the same thing until he wanted to look at something else. Then they would move, very precisely, to focus on the new thing. Even the way he blinked was very exact and at perfectly timed intervals.

I had a robot in my French class and its name was Ben Holly.

'Conjugate!' Frau Blüchner roared. Conjugate is what you do when you are learning a foreign language. Your teacher gives you a verb and you have to give her different forms of that word. In English, for example, if she said 'to walk', you'd have to say 'I walk, you walk, he/she walks, we walk, they walk.

Except this was French, and the word was 'parler' which means to speak. 'Je parle, tu parles, il/elle parle, nous parlons, vous parlez, ils/elles parlent,' I chanted in time with the rest of the class.

Frau Blüchner was actually Mrs Blüchner but we all called her Frau Blüchner. Not to her face though. She taught French and German, although she was actually Dutch. She was about two metres tall, fifty years old, and built like a Panzer tank with an attitude to match. When she said 'conjugate', you conjugated!

She scared the wits out of everyone at school, including, I am sure, the other teachers. All the kids hated her, except, perversely, for me.

I was a bit lazy at my schoolwork, I have to admit. If my homework was ever done on time it was only because I'd stayed up late the night before, doing it all at the last minute. In class I had a habit of losing concentration and staring out of the windows. I couldn't help it. I was easily bored.

But in Frau Blüchner's class I paid attention. Everybody paid attention. Frau Blüchner had a voice that could cut straight through sheet steel and disembowel you from fifty metres away. And, if that didn't work, she had chalk. Chalk ends to be exact. Little left over bullets of chalk that were a bit too small for writing with, so she kept them in a box on her desk.

The one time I had drifted off in French, I had woken up with a smacking sound and a sudden stinging sensation on my face as a chalk bullet caught me square on the cheek. She was a deadly accurate shot.

A parent had once complained to Mr Curtis, the principal, about the chalk. Mr Curtis had invited the parent in for a conference with himself and Frau Blüchner. The story goes that the conference lasted no more than five minutes, after which both the parent and Mr Curtis walked out white-faced, and the matter was closed.

Nobody argues with a Panzer tank.

The day she'd caught me, I'd been watching the birds and thinking about what it would be like to be able to fly. To be light and free, going where you wanted, when you wanted, to be . . . that's when the chalk end got me, and it got me good.

'Care to join us?' Frau Blüchner had asked, in her thick Dutch accent.

'Sorry, Mrs Blüchner,' I had mumbled, and I never let myself lose attention in her class again. I always did my homework too, and put extra effort into my French assignments. Anything to avoid that lashing tongue or those slashing chalk ends.

Today, though, I was in trouble. We'd been given a French song to translate. 'Gentille Alouette', you may know it:

Alouette, gentille Alouette,
Alouette je te plumerai.
Alouette, gentille Alouette,
Alouette je te plumerai.
Je te plumerai la tête,
Je te plumerai la tête,
Et la tête, et la tête,
Alouette, Alouette.
O-o-o-o-oh

It's all about plucking the feathers out of a bird. I'm not sure why you'd want to pluck the feathers out of a bird. It's just an old French folk song. Our homework was to translate the song into an English song. Not just word for word, because that was pretty easy, but to make it rhyme and scan. The problem was, I had been reading a really good book and had put off doing my homework.

Normally, as I said, I would never put off my French homework, but the book was so good I decided that it was too exciting to put down and I would get up early in the morning to do my homework. Good plan. The only problem was, I stayed up so late reading, that the next morning I slept in.

Now I was sitting in Frau Blüchner's class and it was very nearly the end of the period. I was praying that she wasn't going to pick me to read out my song about plucking the feathers out of a bird. I didn't have a song.

Her eyes roamed around the room and eventually settled on me. Probably because of the guilty look on my face.

Don't pick me. I thought desperately at her, the same way I had at Mr Saltham in P.E. *Pick someone else. Don't pick me, don't pick me, don't pick me, don't pick me.*

'Erica,' Frau Blüchner said abruptly to the girl behind me. 'Stand up and read out your song.'

Now is probably a good time to tell you about Erica McDonald. She wasn't all that tall, although she wasn't short, but she was the most extraordinarily beautiful creature I had seen in my life.

Erica was from Scotland, or at least her parents were. I don't know whether she'd been born there, or after they had emigrated to New Zealand, but she had a lovely soft Scottish accent.

Her hair was a kind of a sandy blonde colour and there was a warm, friendly smile always on the verge of shining out from her eyes and mouth. She was smart too. Not like Jane Marks, who was almost as beautiful as Erica but had a vacancy behind her eyes that went on forever.

She sounds perfect doesn't she? And she almost was. But Erica McDonald was the ultimate Ice Queen. I mean she was Frosty the Snow-Girl. Those lips that looked ready to smile never did. She clearly thought she was a bit too good for the rest of us, and kept to herself as much as possible. She had a boyfriend (according to the school grapevine), a senior at Rosmini College. I'd had her in my class nearly a whole year and I don't think I'd spoken to her once. Which was partly me, of course, but mostly her. She wouldn't speak to the likes of me. Yet I still had a crush on her, in an 'it'll never happen' sort of way.

'Stand up and read out your song,' said Frau Blüchner. As Erica got to her feet, I found myself wondering why Frau Blüchner had not picked me. Could it possibly be I had changed her mind? I was certain she had been staring directly at me. Or had she been staring over my shoulder at Erica the whole time?

Was it possible that, somehow by projecting my thoughts as strongly as I could at Frau Blüchner's brain, I had implanted the thought into her mind? It seemed even more unlikely than my theory about Ben being a robot. And yet when you thought about that time in PE . . .

Erica finished and sat down. Frau Blüchner just nodded and said quietly, 'All right.' This was high praise from her.

The bell still hadn't gone for end of period, and the teacher moved back to the blackboard and paused, thinking for a moment. More conjugation coming up, I thought, and wondered what word it would be. An odd thought popped into my mind and I focused on Frau Blüchner's head and concentrated over and over again on a single word.

Knickers, I thought. There was no way Frau Blüchner was going to write *knickers* on the blackboard. It wasn't even a French word. But if she wrote *knickers* it would prove my (unlikely) theory. *Knickers, knickers, knickers, knickers, knickers,* I thought. She reached down and absent-mindedly picked up a piece of chalk. There was a cough from the back of the class and she looked around, distracted by the sound.

Then, as if in a daze, she wrote a 'K' then an 'N', followed by an 'I'.

Knickers, Frau Blüchner wrote on the blackboard as if it was a common French verb. She slammed the chalk down on the chalk tray and turned back to the class.

'Conjugate,' she said.

Nobody said anything. I suspect they were all too stunned and, anyway, you can't conjugate an English noun in French, so nobody knew what to do. In another teacher's class there would have been muffled sniggering. But not in Frau Blüchner's.

As for me, I was the most surprised of all and more than a little bewildered at what had just happened. It seemed I had somehow made Frau Blüchner write the word *knickers* on the blackboard just by thinking about it.

'Conjugate!' Frau Blüchner roared, but still there was silence. Her face began to go red, a sure sign of an explosion building, but still nobody said anything. What was there to say? Her eyes flicked around the room, looking for a victim. They settled on her son.

Frau Blüchner's son was named Markus Blüchner, but we all called him Blocker. Yeah, that Blocker. Actually I called him Blockhead, but not to his face. He'd beaten up kids for far less than that. He called me Freak. To my face. Not that any of the teachers would know anything about that. As far as the teachers were concerned he was a hero. The star of the league team. A try-scoring prop-forward, a polite and gentle giant. Teachers can be so blind. In reality, he was heavy, strong and a merciless bully.

Blocker got no special treatment in his mother's French class. I suspected he got a harder time than most, just to show us, or him, that he was getting no favours. So, it was no surprise that she picked him to conjugate. Unfortunately for Blocker the word was not conjugateable.

'But …' Blocker began, trying desperately to figure a way out of this one.

'I didn't ask for *buts*, I asked you to conjugate!'

I wondered if she was like that at home. It might explain a bit about Blocker.

Blocker was still silent.

'Conjugate!'

Eventually he stuttered, 'Je knicker, tu knickers, il/elle knicker.'

The rest of the class froze. You know that feeling when you desperately want to burst out into giggles, but you dare not. Jenny Kreisler, sitting to my right, clapped both hands over her mouth. I suppose I was the only one who wasn't inwardly cracking up. I was still too flabbergasted.

Ben the robot, a few seats in front of me, had no such constraint. He was actually shaking as he struggled to hold in his laughter. I guess his humour circuits were getting overloaded.

Blocker's mother went purple. Blocker didn't stop; he just tried to do his best. Even getting it wrong was preferable to not trying, I suppose.

'Nous knickons, vous knickez, ils/elles knickent,' he finished.

The volcano was building, and I braced myself for the eruption, when all of a sudden Frau Blüchner turned and looked at the board, and all the steam went out of her as if someone had popped a release valve.

'Who wrote …' she started to say, but stopped, because she knew that it was her.

She stood there for a while, shaking her head uncomprehendingly. Then she marched to the blackboard and scraped the offending word off with a duster, before writing up naître (to be born).

At that point two things happened. The bell went for the

end of class and Ben Holly erupted into a fit of giggles. His programmers needed to work on that. Frau Blüchner turned and glared at him but said nothing.

Ben was just about falling out of his chair, and that set off the rest of the class. Most of them tried to contain it until they were safely clear of the danger zone that was French class. Then they burst into uncontrollable laughter.

Not Blocker though. The evil eye he gave little Ben Holly was enough to slice through flesh and bone. Most of the class had been laughing but Ben had started it, and I knew that he was in for a beating at lunchtime. I hoped it wouldn't damage any of his circuits.

I'm still not sure what made Blocker so malevolent just then. Was it because he thought Ben was laughing at him? Or was it because he thought Ben was laughing at his mother?

Either way, Ben Holly was in for a hiding. And I was in for a lot of thinking.

6

GWF

Blocker didn't wait until lunchtime. He waylaid Ben in the stairwell, pinning him against the wire-reinforced glass of the floor-to-ceiling windows.

The clatter of kids' feet continued below the landing, but those of us coming down stopped as a knob of kids bunched up to watch Ben get the snot kicked out of him.

There were six or seven kids in front of me, so it seemed I was going to have to watch as well.

I didn't want to. I was feeling uncommonly guilty. It hadn't been Ben's fault really, it had been mine. If I hadn't made Frau Blüchner write *knickers* on the board, then Ben wouldn't be about to get his teeth smashed in.

'Something funny in class?' big, sneering Blocker Blüchner asked little Ben Holly, knowing he wouldn't answer.

Ben just shook his head, terrified.

'Here's a good joke,' Blocker said, and punched Ben in the stomach, hard.

Ben gasped and doubled up, clutching at his midriff.

'You'll split your sides,' Blocker said and drew back his fist for another strike.

I couldn't do anything. It just wasn't fair. I aimed all my attention at the back of Blocker's head and thought furiously *Leave him alone, you big ugly ape. Leave him alone, you big ugly ape.*

Blocker paused, one arm drawn back, and I slammed the thought again and again into his brain. *Leave him alone, you big ugly ape!*

Then, to my horror, Blocker slowly turned and looked directly at me. To my even greater horror I saw the other kids were turning too, with looks of disbelief. Urgently I replayed my mental videotape of the last few seconds and realized, to my immense fright, that I had been concentrating so hard I had said the words out loud!

'What did you say, Freak?' Blocker asked, unable to believe that someone would be stupid enough to say such a thing.

Nothing! I wanted to scream. *I didn't say anything!* But it was far too late for that. 'Leave him alone,' I said out loud, and added 'Blockhead.' What did I have to lose?

Blocker moved towards me, pushing through the crowd of kids gathered on the stairs but, just at that moment, the sound of a door closing came from the classroom above us. Frau Blüchner was on her way down. The kids quickly started to disperse, and Blocker stopped where he was.

'I'm going to get you, Freak,' he said, in a voice that was as low as it was deadly and punctuated with a stabbing finger in my direction.

Out of nowhere another bizarre thought popped into my head and, without stopping to think, I said, 'You think you're so tough, I'll take you on. I'll take you on at GWF!'

There was a gasp from the crowd, and Blocker's eyes widened in surprise.

'You're on, Freak,' he said with a malicious sneer. 'You are so dead.'

'OK, then,' I said, wondering why kids like Blocker always spoke in such terrible clichés. 'But in the meantime, try not to be so noisome.'

While he tried to work out what that meant, I pushed through the crowd, and walked, much more casually than I felt, past Blocker. I wasn't feeling all that clever though, because unless I could come up with something, and fast, I was shortly going to be turned into mincemeat by the toughest son-of-a-bum in year nine.

A hand caught me by the arm as I walked out of G block, and I whirled around, expecting a fight. But it was Erica.

'You did a good thing,' she said in that beautiful burr of an accent, and, for the first time, I saw the smile that was bubbling just below the surface. Just for a brief flash. Then the Ice Queen was back and, before I could say anything, she was off, gliding down the path towards F block.

Ben came and stood by me as I watched Erica walk away. He was rubbing his stomach and looking a bit confused.

'Why did you stick up for me?' he asked in his perfectly controlled, but quite realistic sounding, artificial voice.

'No reason,' I said. There was no way of explaining it.

'Well, thanks,' he said, and the way he said it conveyed such emotion that I found myself wondering if he really was a robot. Maybe it was all the stress of the moment or maybe it was something else but, normally, I never would have said what I said next.

'Are you a robot?' I asked, and winced, realizing how silly it sounded.

'What!?' Ben gave me a funny look. Once started though, I had to continue.

'Are you a real kid, or are you a robot?'

'I'm a kid,' Ben said emphatically. 'A real kid.'

'Well, you walk like a robot.'

There was silence while he digested this.

'Do I?' he asked at last.

'Yeah. Are you sure you're not a robot? Maybe your creators wouldn't tell you. Maybe they'd want you to think you were a real kid.'

'Oh.' Ben looked more and more confused. 'Right. I hadn't thought of that. How would we tell?'

I thought for a moment, then said, 'We could cut one of your arms open, and see if there's wires and stuff inside.'

'Ouch,' said Ben, quite calmly really, considering what I was suggesting. 'But what if you were wrong? There'd be blood everywhere.'

'Yeah, I suppose.'

We started to head down the path, in the same direction as Erica.

'Do you have a mum and dad?' I asked, thinking he might live in a laboratory or something.

'Yes,' Ben said. 'Just like other kids.'

'Are there any photos of you as a baby?' It would be a dead giveaway if there weren't.

But Ben said, 'Yes, just like other kids.'

'And what happens when you go home after school?' I asked, still searching for clues.

'Nothing,' he said. 'I go home, do my homework, then go to bed and Mum plugs me into the charger for the night, just like other kids.'

I turned and stared at him in shock, and it took me a moment or two to realize he was joking.

Then Ben Holly walked alongside me to physics class, and we got to talking a bit more. I kind of liked his sense of humour and realised that I'd better be careful or I'd end up having a friend.

GWF stands for Glenfield Wrestling Federation. It's not a federation at all. It's just a bunch of stupid kids ripping off those wrestling shows on TV.

The biggest, thuggiest kids in the school run it. Year elevens mainly. I suppose years twelve and thirteen have outgrown the whole wrestling thing.

They run the wrestling on Fridays after school, in the school boxing ring.

Not many schools have a boxing ring, so I guess we were lucky, or unlucky, depending on your point of view. Old Sea Salt had been a champion boxer in his day, and he'd somehow persuaded the principal, the Board of Trustees and whoever else needed to be persuaded, that it was good for fitness and self-defence.

It served just as well as a wrestling ring and the kids who were into that would bash the crap out of each other using moves borrowed from the TV and for some reason think it was fun.

I heard that they almost had to stop it a couple of years ago when one of them broke his arm. But the kid never told his parents or any teachers what really happened, so they just kept it quiet for a few weeks then carried on as usual.

And I, stupid idiot me, was going to get into the ring with big bully Blocker Blüchner, who was hell-bent on my destruction, unless I could find some way to weasel out of it.

As Homer Simpson once said, 'It's important to learn to weasel out of things. That's what separates man from the animals, (except the weasel).'

My new friend Ben had some ideas on how to weasel out of things. For a start, this coming Friday was the last day of term so the GWF kids weren't holding a match.

That meant it would be at least three weeks before the first GWF match in the new term.

Ben thought I should spend those weeks at a boxing gym, or karate lessons, learning to defend myself. I felt that I was unlikely to learn enough in three weeks to defend myself against a monster like Blocker.

I wondered if there was some way to use my strange new power to win the fight, but I couldn't see how it would help when he was body-slamming me and smashing me into the floor of the ring.

As far as I could work out, I had about three weeks left to live.

1

My Dad

You know my dad.

I mean, not personally, but you'd know my dad if you saw him. If I stuck a picture of him here . . .☺ . . . you'd go, 'Oh yeah, that's the guy from the . . . commercial.' The commercial you stuck in the gap would depend on what you were into. If you were into chocolate, for example, you'd go, 'The guy from the Cadbury commercial.' Or if you were into rugby you'd say, 'The guy from the All Black Supporters commercial.' If you were into dogs you'd go, 'He's the policeman from the dog food commercial.' It's funny but after that commercial came out, a lot of people thought my dad really was a policeman. He's not, of course. He's just a sometimes employed actor. When Mum and Dad are fighting, she calls him an unemployed bum. Which is kind of funny, because you know that ad with the builder who whips off his tool belt and his pants fall down? That's my dad too. You can't see his face, but you can see his bum. So I guess he's not always an unemployed bum. Sometimes he's a working bum!

But, back to the dog food commercial. It's the really funny one where the burglar has stolen a case of dog food and the police dog chases him. Then the burglar drops the case and all the cans spill out but, instead of chasing him, the dog just tries to open one of the cans. It's really funny.

I guess you had to be there.

Dad wasn't always an actor. When we lived in the South Island he was a radio announcer. That was why we shifted so often. They move around a lot, radio announcers. Then, when the radio station in Wellington where he worked was bought out by some big network and he lost his job, he decided to move to Auckland to make his fortune in acting.

There were TV commercials, film roles, bit parts on TV shows and, of course, the ultimate for any wannabe actor in New Zealand, the chance of a regular role on *Shortland Street*. The possibilities seemed endless.

The reality of Auckland was small roles in several movies, on a pittance of a pay rate (*but I'm getting to meet all the important people in the industry!*), quite a few TV commercials and a couple of walk-on parts in TV shows.

Not quite what Dad was hoping for from his career I think. Some of the jobs were well paid. The only problem was they didn't happen frequently enough. As Mum pointed out whenever they had an argument, he could be earning more each year as a checkout operator at the supermarket. But, as Dad always pointed back, the acting stuff might lead on to something bigger, whereas the supermarket job wouldn't.

So, we never had any money and lived in a rented house and had constant fights with the landlord over paying the rent late. We didn't have a car or new clothes for us kids. But we always ate a good meal. Mum made sure of that. I'm sure she sometimes borrowed money from her parents, because, somehow, there was always food in the cupboards.

I sat on the old sofa in the lounge and stared at Gumbo, thinking thoughts into his brain.

I don't know what kind of dog Gumbo was. I don't think he was any kind of dog really, just a mixture of all-sorts which had resulted in a large, yellow-brown creature with a squat, bear-like face and sorrowful eyes. His fur was long, and his favourite activity was flopping all over people and slobbering on them. He was just a big lovable rug of a dog. A floppy, sloppy dog, and we had had him since I was born.

Sit! I thought. *Sit! Sit, sit, sit, sit, sit, sit, sit!*

He stared at me with his big sad eyes but didn't even try to sit.

Ok, I thought, *roll over. Roll over, roll over, roll over.*

Gumbo blinked at me and sat.

I kept trying for the next half hour, but nothing much happened. Then Gumbo did a really bad fart so I sent him out to the garage where his basket was and opened the windows to let in some fresh air.

I heard Mum's key in the front door then, which gave me a new guinea pig. I started on her before she even walked into the room.

Pizza for dinner tonight, pizza for dinner tonight, pizza for dinner tonight.

It was a bit mean. I knew she'd be tired from a day spent cleaning other people's houses, and wouldn't really feel like cooking tea, but pizza is quite expensive. It was a rare treat in our house. So it was a bit unfair of me, I suppose.

But I really liked pizza.

Pizza for dinner tonight, pizza for dinner tonight.

I jumped up when she walked in the lounge and gave her a big smile.

'G'day, mate,' she smiled back tiredly. 'How was school?'

'Same old,' I said. *Pizza for dinner tonight!*

'Where's your sister?' Mum asked.

I pointed to April's room and made a telephone out of my finger and thumb. We looked at each other and laughed. My sister was *always* on the phone.

Mum went into the kitchen without mentioning anything about pizza, but I noticed that she didn't start cooking anything either.

Dad came in about 4:30 after a day of doing the voice-over for a TV commercial for shampoo. He looked excited, vibrant, alive. I suppose it was a different kind of work to scrubbing bathrooms and vacuuming all day.

April finally got off the phone at about 6:15, when the pizza arrived.

8

What I did in the Holidays

It was drizzling the first Saturday of the holidays. One of those grey miserable days that make you feel like crying even if you are happy. And, lying on my bed trying not to think about GWF (and failing), I wasn't particularly happy. Every now and then I'd stop worrying about that and start wondering what I was going to do with my strange new power.

I felt I could become some kind of super-hero, like Batman or the Masked Avenger. Use my special power to save the world. Or at least save a few people. From exactly what I was going to save them, I wasn't sure.

When the phone rang, and Mum said it was for me, I was surprised. Nobody rang me up. Except Nana One on my birthday. Sometimes Nana Two, when she remembered.

It was Ben.

'I reckon I know how you can get out of the GWF,' he said in that flat controlled tone of his. 'I've got a plan.'

A weasel out plan.

'Do you want to come around?' I asked. 'The Warriors are playing at Ericsson this afternoon. We could watch, if you like. Daniel's playing.'

Thirteen-year-old Daniel Taylor went to our school and was the youngest ever player on the Warriors Rugby League team. He'd been on the reserves' bench for a couple of games, but had not yet run on to the field. Maybe today would be the day.

'Um, I'd have to ask Mum,' Ben said, but arrived on a bicycle, in a bright yellow raincoat, about twenty minutes later.

'Cool posters,' he said when I showed him my room. I had posters around the walls, mainly of space stuff like a giant close-up photo of the moon on which all the craters were named in small black type, and one of the space shuttle Columbia, inset with photos of the astronauts who died.

'Yeah,' I said. 'You into space?'

'Yeah,' he nodded. 'Since I was ten. I've got a really cool poster of Apollo Eleven, the whole rocket, that's over two metres tall. It stretches from the floor right up to the ceiling.'

'Wow,' I said enviously, 'that's big.'

We started to talk some more about space stuff, but it all went straight out of the window with a shuffling, scratching noise on the particleboard floor of the hallway, and I braced myself for the onslaught.

Gumbo, the big floppy, sloppy dog, burst into the room like a tornado and headed straight for Ben. Ben actually shrieked a little with fright as Gumbo leapt up on to him, knocking him backwards on to the bed, and slobbering all over him. Which was Gumbo's way of saying hello.

Once Ben had got used to Gumbo, he seemed to like him. And vice-versa, which was strange. I mean Gumbo liked everyone, but they were such opposites: Ben, the neat precise robot-person with his tidy appearance and clinical movements, and Gumbo the … well … the floppy, sloppy dog.

Ben told me he had always wanted a dog, but his mother

wouldn't allow one in the house. Too smelly. Too messy. Too noisy. I thought those were some of the best things about a dog. But I guess everyone is different.

After all the commotion died down, I said, 'So how am I going to weasel out of getting my brains scrambled, mashed and fried, by Blocker the Blockhead in the GWF ring?'

'Well, you shouldn't have got yourself in this situation in the first place, if you ask me,' Ben said, straight-faced.

I laughed. We both knew that if I hadn't got myself into this situation he would be a smear on the toughened glass of the G-Block stairwell by now.

'Maybe I could change schools,' I said. 'I've done that plenty of times.' I wasn't serious. Even saying those words out loud made a cold, clawing sensation travel the length of my body. I *couldn't* go through the whole new school thing again.

Ben shook his head, taking my suggestion seriously. 'Zoning regulations. Your parents would have to move house.'

'Unless I got myself expelled,' I said, semi-seriously.

'You've got two choices,' Ben said. 'You can fight him …'

'And get pulverized.'

'Or you can spend the rest of your years at high school trying to hide from him.'

Neither option sounded viable to me.

I said, 'So what's your great plan then?'

'We break your arm.'

'What!?'

'Seriously. If your arm is broken, then you can't fight him, can you? And by the time your arm is better, he'll have forgotten all about it.'

'I'm not so sure,' I said sourly. 'And how do you plan to break my arm anyway?'

42

'Well,' Ben said thoughtfully, 'you could fall off your bike, but I suppose you might end up doing a lot of other injuries to yourself at the same time, and there's no guarantee of breaking the bone you want to break.'

'Hmmm,' I said doubtfully. 'What if we just pretended to break my arm?'

Ben shook his head. 'If your arm wasn't in a proper cast, Blocker would know you were faking.' He thought for a moment. 'Has your dad got a vice?'

'Yeah, he has a whole workshop set up in the garage.'

When he wasn't acting, Dad was mending furniture for people; a skill he had picked up somewhere along the way. There was plenty of room in the garage as we didn't own a car.

'Well, we could stick your arm in the vice, then I could hit it with a sledge hammer,' Ben suggested cheerfully.

'You have got to be kidding.'

'Be better than getting the pudding punched out of you by Blocker.'

'But how would we explain it to my parents?'

'Well, we could say you fell off your bike.'

We spent the next half hour discussing ways to break my arm (my left arm, not my right arm, we decided, so that it wouldn't interfere with schoolwork). Maybe I was chicken, or maybe I just wasn't sure that Blocker would drop the whole thing if I couldn't fight him for a few more weeks. Either way, I couldn't summon up a whole lot of enthusiasm for the idea. Still, it was nice of Ben to try and help.

A sledge hammer and a vice!?

Mum was out at a cleaning job. Dad was at his agent's. So April, my obnoxious big sister, was babysitting me again. She was the one who needed baby-sitting if you asked me, but nobody ever did. We watched the Warriors' game, which was a waste of time, because Daniel just sat on the bench for the entire game. Gumbo watched with us. He always liked watching rugby or rugby league on TV; although I don't think he was too hot on the rules. He just lay there and barked occasionally when the crowd were roaring, and farted a lot.

Gumbo, the farty, sporty, floppy, sloppy dog.

By the time the game finished it was six o'clock, so Ben rang his mum and asked if he could stay for dinner.

April had been left in charge of dinner. That turned out to be cheese on toast. April, sixteen-years-old, only knew how to make one meal, and that was cheese on toast. It wasn't that I didn't like cheese on toast, but you would have thought she could have used a little more imagination.

Straight after dinner she hopped on the phone to her boyfriend, and I knew she'd be there all night.

'Where are your mum and dad?' Ben asked during dinner.

'Mum's working and Dad's gone to his agent's house for dinner. Dad's on *Crime Time* tonight.'

Ben looked blank.

'That TV show where they ask for the public's help to solve crimes.'

'What did he do?' Ben asked, wide-eyed.

I laughed. 'Nothing! He's an actor. They're doing a reconstruction of the robbery last week at the Orewa TAB. Dad's playing the part of the Hunchback Robber.'

'Cool!'

I shook my head. 'You won't even be able to recognize him, because he'll be wearing the mask the whole time.'

The Hunchback Robber had been hitting places for months

around the upper North Island: TAB's, shops, post offices, even a Plunket collection centre. He was a terrifying sight, apparently, in a gruesome Quasimodo mask, wearing a black raincoat, and his back had a huge hump. Each time the police were on the scene within minutes, yet the robber had somehow vanished. Dad had landed the role of playing him on *Crime Time*. He wasn't too happy because, while it paid well, it did nothing for his profile as his face would not be seen.

The afternoon's drizzle had turned into heavy rain by evening; bucketing down against our tin roof.

Ben had brought his digital camera around, and we played with that for a while, then played games on his mobile phone until *Crime Time* started.

His phone had much better games than my old thing.

Even April watched the programme, although she stayed on the phone to her boyfriend the whole time, discussing the show so loudly with him that we could hardly hear what the presenter was saying.

The presenter was a real cop. Or at least an ex-cop. He wore a police uniform, and they called him Sergeant Wilkinson as if he was still on the force. Sternly, he introduced several minor crimes, showing police photos of the offenders, while building up to the main story about the Hunchback Robber.

Our curtains suddenly lit up as lightning, and then thunder, were added into the recipe of the storm outside. A sudden fuzziness blurted across the TV screen. We had a big flash TV, which did look a bit out of place in our litle house. I explained to Ben that Dad needed it for his job. He often had to watch videos of his work, or from some of the acting workshops he went on.

At the moment the screen was filled with the weather-worn

face of Sergeant Wilkinson. He might have been a real policeman and probably a good one but, as a presenter, he was useless. He had this dull dry way of talking that made even the most exciting crime sound like a discussion about floral arranging at some old-folks' tea party.

Ben called him PC Plod, and I thought that was outrageously funny for some reason.

Finally, Dad's item came on the show, and even April stopped talking while she watched, although she didn't hang up.

There was another flash of lightning outside and the screen went all fuzzy again, but it came back after a couple of seconds.

Sergeant Wilkinson droned on for a few moments, surely the only presenter in the world who could make the terrifying Hunchback Robber sound boring. Then Dad came on the screen, in a black raincoat, the hump above his right shoulder and the Quasimodo mask making him look like a demented clown. He raced into the TAB and started waving a sawn-off shotgun around wildly.

Don't overdo it, Dad, I thought to myself, but said nothing out loud.

Dad – the Hunchback Robber – raced out into the street and, in an unusually arty bit of film work for this kind of show, slowly dissolved into nothing as he ran down the main street of Orewa.

'And, as usual,' Sergeant Wilkinson droned, 'the Hunchback Robber just vanished into thin air.'

Ben and I applauded Dad's performance, while April just went back to her chatter. My mind was busy, though. Something about the way they had made the robber disappear. As if he was some kind of super-criminal. He wasn't a super-criminal though, he was just a thug. Now if it had been me . . . with my special power . . . hmmm.

'That lightning is getting closer,' Ben said as there was another flash. 'Do you want to come up to the power pylon on Manuka Ridge?'

I stared at him, and April paused and looked at him curiously.

'Why?' I asked.

'You're not going out anywhere,' April said shortly, and went back to her conversation.

Ben said, 'It's the highest thing around for miles. It attracts lightning like a magnet. It's pretty spectacular.'

'You're not going out anywhere in this storm,' April said again, playing Mother and scarcely breaking into her phone call to do so.

Up till that point, the idea of going out into a raging storm to watch lightning had been the last thing I wanted to do. But once my annoying sister had outlawed it . . . well, that changed everything.

'You're not the boss of me,' I said angrily.

'I am while Mum and Dad are out.'

She somehow seemed to be able to carry on two conversations at once.

'I'm going.'

'No, you're not.'

Ben shrugged, and shook his head silently. *It's not worth it,* he was saying.

I narrowed my eyes and stared at April. She was blabbering on about some friend of hers at school. It wasn't fair. She could do whatever she wanted and I always had to do what other people told me to do.

47

I pictured her brain sitting inside her head. Actually, to be truthful, I pictured it as about the size of a plum, which was probably a little unfair. I'm sure it was at least the size of a grapefruit.

I waited for a gap in her conversation, until she was getting ready to speak. Then I painted in vivid flashes across her (plum-sized) brain.

Let's get married. Let's get married. Let's get married.

'Let's get married,' April said suddenly into the phone. Just as suddenly she turned bright red and nearly dropped the phone. I could just about hear the shocked silence at the other end of the line.

'Um. I don't mean.' It was hilarious; I'd never seen her so flustered. 'I'm not sure why I said it . . . No really. I didn't . . . I mean . . . well . . .'

I left her trying to wriggle out of that and motioned to Ben. She didn't even notice us as we left.

9

The Lightning Tower

Ben had a really cool torch. One of those long black ones like security guards carry. His was made by Smith & Wesson, who I thought made guns; it looked a bit like a gun. It was heavy as anything and I wondered why he carried it around in his backpack, but didn't ask.

I grabbed Dad's yellow torch from the garage. The torch was clipped to a peg-board with all of his tools. Every tool had a place, neatly outlined in black ink so you would know where to put it back once you had used it. I flashed the torch on quickly to make sure it worked (it did, barely), then unlocked the back garage door.

Gumbo whined at me, wanting to come, but just then another searing flash of lightning lit up the windows of the garage, and I swear he went white as a ghost and disappeared back into the house whimpering.

'Chicken!' I called after him, not feeling so brave myself.

The wind whipped the door out of my hand as I went to close it behind us and slammed it shut, almost taking my fingers off in the process. The whole house seemed to shake with the impact. Then there was another brilliant flash of light followed a few seconds later by a huge peal of thunder, and this time the house really did shake. I could see the image of the streetlights in the garage windows dissolve into a million fractured pieces, like a reflection in a pool of water after you have tossed in a pebble.

'Are you sure you want to go out in this?' I asked Ben, but he was busy looking at his watch, huddled into his rain coat as if trying to hide from the weather. His coat was really cool, with fluoro strips, like those the cops wear.

'Three seconds,' he said. 'That means it's just a few kilometres away, and still getting closer. We'll have to hurry.'

He trotted off into the storm, the light from his flashlight cutting a laser beam through the rain, and called back over his shoulder, 'You can't photograph a lightning strike on a fine day!'

We were at the top of the hill when lightning flashed again, and from here we could just see the tip of the pylon jutting above the dark trees, silhouetted against the brilliant, but momentary, blaze of light.

'Hurry up!' Ben called, metres in front of me, but easily visible in his bright coat. I grabbed the tip of my hood and pulled it low over my face. Even so, the pelting rain found its way inside and ran down the sides of my neck.

Ben seemed to relish it all, turning his face into the rain and cackling like an old witch. I just kept thinking that water must have somehow found its way into his circuits, and his system was going haywire.

It wasn't until we reached the bus shelter on the corner of Ridge Road that I saw what Ben was up to.

It was a bus shelter with glass walls and an opening which

faced the massive structure of the pylon. The weather was blowing against the back of the shelter, so it was a huge relief to step into some relative warmth and dryness.

Across the road, in the middle of a cleared field, the power pylon impassively faced the weather, impervious to its effects. It was huge. One of the mighty soldiers carrying the high voltage wires across the countryside and down to the Glenfield substation. It started at a four-cornered base and, a little like the Eiffel tower, narrowed as it stretched towards the sky. Near the top, three hefty arms reached out from either side, gripping tightly to the lines with huge ridged insulators.

The wires were almost invisible against the dark sky, except where they passed close to streetlights. There, the sheen of the lights on the wires made rhythmical dancing patterns against the blackness of the sky.

It gave me an odd feeling, watching the pylon. It was strong, masterful, brimming with energy and power, yet, at the same time, strangely powerless. It had no say in its own destiny. It had no free will. It just stood there and did its job, facing the elements.

'How do you know the lightning's going to strike the pylon tonight?' I asked, shouting over the booming of the rain against the glass wall behind us.

'I don't,' Ben replied. 'But it's the highest thing for miles around, and the lightning's really close. So it's good odds.'

'Have you done this before?' I asked incredulously.

'Five times,' he said. 'But I've never got a photo yet.'

Lightning flashed again and the thunder followed almost immediately.

'Got to hurry,' Ben said. 'It's right on top of us!' He pulled a tiny metal shape out of his backpack and unfolded it into a full-sized tripod. He had all the toys, that boy. His parents must have been loaded. I didn't even have an ordinary camera.

'Why not?' I asked, as he screwed his camera on to the top of the device.

'Why not what?'

'Why didn't you get the photo?'

'Four times the lightning didn't strike the tower, and the other time it did but I missed the shot.'

I shone my torch on his face and he grinned at me. 'Sixth time lucky!'

'But how do you know when to take the photo?'

'I don't. I just set the camera on a low aperture and leave the shutter open for half a minute at a time.'

As he spoke, he lined the camera up at the pylon, making a few adjustments, and pressed the shutter button.

I stared at the camera in silence for a long moment, until it finally clicked off. Ben immediately pressed the button again and, even as he did so, there was a searing flash of light that seemed to be all around us, turning night into day and, at the same moment, an enormous explosion of thunder rattled the glass panels of the bus shelter so violently I was afraid they would shatter.

I thought the world had erupted. I thought I had been caught in the middle of an explosion. I thought I was dead.

Ben, on the other hand, was just about jumping out of his skin. 'I think I got it! I think I got it!'

'Can't you check?' I said in a kind of daze, my ears still ringing from the explosion.

He shook his head, and I realized that he had already

pressed the shutter again. 'I'm taking another in case it happens again.'

'But I thought lightning never strikes in the same place twice.'

Ben laughed. 'Lightning strikes at the tallest object. It'll hit the tower again unless it has already moved too far away.'

There was another flash of light and a roaring freight train of thunder, but this came from further down the valley and seemed a bit less like the end of the world.

Ben nodded. 'It's passed by. Let's have a look then.'

He wound the camera off the tripod, breathless with excitement, and pressed a couple of buttons on the back.

The pylon flashed up on the little screen, soaring into the night sky, a towering pattern of black rods, silhouetted in the light of the jagged streak of heaven that speared it from above. It was awesome, breathtaking. The lightning bolt itself was a multi-fingered river of light, jagged and deadly, frozen in a split second of time on Ben's camera.

What a contrast! The pylon: powerful, yet powerless. The lightning bolt: sleek and deadly, free to roam the sky, obeying no rules, striking where and when it pleased.

'Wow,' I said slowly, comprehending for the first time what the struggle up the steep road in the storm had been all about. 'Wow!'

Ben was beaming in the light of my torch. 'We got it, we got it!'

It occurred to me that he had included me in his excitement. I had done nothing, and yet I was still part of the success. I guess that's what friends are all about.

I turned and stared down over the hillside. The lightning flashed another time, still nearby, and the brilliance of it illuminated all the dark recesses of my mind, giving me a sudden clarity, throwing thoughts into stark relief.

At that moment I knew, beyond doubt, what to do with my strange and unique power.

10

The Dream

Spending school holidays with a friend was infinitely more fun than spending them alone. I had known that, once upon a time but, somehow, I had forgotten it.

I had planned to read Isaac Asimov's Foundation trilogy during the break, but got less than halfway through. Instead, Ben and I spent the whole time playing, exploring, riding bikes, and trying to think of ways to outwit Blocker and save my life.

We would text each other to work out where to meet up.

Of course, Ben's cellphone was much more flash than mine. His was a really cool new one, with changeable face-plates, polyphonic ringtones and a built in camera.

Mine was a three-times hand-me-down. It had been Dad's originally, then Mum's, then April's, and only then, the next time Dad upgraded his phone, did I get it. It was old and clunky; I wasn't allowed to make calls on it unless it was an emergency. But it was OK for text.

Those holidays were the best of my life, despite the threat of Blocker hanging over my head.

The Sunday night before term began, I woke up in the middle of the night, sweating.

It took me a moment to realize where I was. The dream had seemed so real.

I had dreamed I was an electron, whizzing along one of those high-voltage power lines. Completely powerless to do anything but follow the path of the wire. Unable to stop, go back, or change course. It was a path I couldn't predict, didn't understand, and had no control over.

Then the dream changed and, instead of a wire, it was a travelator, the one at the Glenfield Mall, except it was bright red. I was on it, and waiting for me at the other end was Blocker, grinning evilly as the travelator carried me slowly, but unavoidably, towards him.

I looked back, and Erica McDonald was standing there, aloof, icy. Gradually getting smaller and smaller.

Then the travelator suddenly turned into a giant pavlova with raspberries, and I woke up.

I don't know why dreams do that.

11

First Crime

Life is a bit like a book, if you ask me.

The first page is when you are born and the last page is when you die. In between are a whole bunch of chapters: some good and some bad; some funny and some sad.

The way I coped when things weren't going well was by saying to myself, 'Don't worry, the next chapter will be better.' And somehow it always was.

But this particular chapter in my life was turning out to be one of the worst. In fact, it was a nightmare. First week back at school and everywhere I turned I seemed to run into Blocker or one of his mates: in the corridors; outside the school gate in the morning; even just harmlessly walking across the top field. There they were, Blocker or Phil Domane or Emilio, the other empty-headed thug that he hung out with. They didn't touch me. They just smirked, or sneered evilly at me.

On Wednesday at lunchtime my mobile phone beeped with a text message. It was just Mum telling me she would be late home. But I looked up from reading the message to see Blocker and his mates killing themselves laughing in front of me.

'Is that a mobile phone or a brick?' Blocker guffawed.

Phil contributed, 'Does it run on electricity? Or do you have to keep shovelling coal in somewhere?'

My phone was old and a bit big, but not *that* big. I shoved it away in my bag and ignored them.

Before too long I would be laughing at their mobile phones, because I would have the latest, smallest model available. I was going to be rich, rich and powerful. I would be the lightning bolt, not the power pylon.

I was going to become a villain. And not just any villain. I would become a super-villain, like those in the comic books. Not some lame super-hero and not some thug like the Hunchback Robber.

With my power I could do what I wanted. Get whatever I wanted. A digital camera, a cool tripod thing. Anything.

A super-villain. That was me. I had the power. I had the desire. I just needed a name. And maybe a costume, although I wasn't too sure about that part, especially if it involved wearing my undies on the outside of my clothes!

All super-villains have names. Batman had The Riddler and the Joker to deal with. Superman had Lex Luthor and Austin Powers had Dr Evil. That's what I needed; a cool evil name so that I could leave little cryptic messages for the police to decipher as I embarked on my life of crime. I kept my mind working on it. It took my thoughts away from other things.

I had already planned my first crime. Nothing fancy. Just a simple little deed to test out my powers and make sure I could get away with it. Something that, if I was caught, would not land me in jail, or get me expelled from school. That thought terrified me. I had been through so many schools in such a short time; the thought of another shift was unbearable.

I planned the crime in the school library, sitting at a long wooden table by myself. There wasn't a lot to plan, but I knew that master criminals planned their crimes carefully. I planned mine with an encyclopaedia of New Zealand wildlife open in front of me so it would look like I was studying. My eyes were on a takahe but my mind was in the school tuck shop.

The school tuck shop sold pies and chips, soft drinks and ice blocks, sausage rolls and rockets and all kinds of other food that I was generally not allowed except on very special occasions because of the numbers.

What numbers?

The numbers.

Next time you pick up a bottle of soft drink or an ice block or some kind of pre-packaged food, turn it over and have a look at the ingredients. You'll see sugar, lecithin, cocoa, peanuts and all sorts of things that they put into convenience food for kids. And, usually, you'll see a few numbers. The list will look something like this:

Contains: Sugar, lecithin, wheat, sesame seed oil, 436, 328, cocoa, peanuts.

About two years earlier my mum had discovered numbers. Numbers were chemicals, and heaven only knew what effect those chemicals were having on children today. I think she imagined future generations of kids with two heads, who glow in the dark.

If it was the sort of ingredient that didn't have a name, only a number, then it wasn't going in my mouth, according to my mum. Which pretty much put the tuck shop off limits.

So, this was my first crime. The great tuck shop raid.

Most of my planning wasn't about how I was going to commit the crime. It was how I was going to get away with it, and particularly how I was going to act if I got caught out. Like it was all a big mistake. *Oh, did I do that? I wasn't thinking. Didn't have my head screwed on straight today.*

On Wednesday, the day of the tuck shop raid, I took my packed lunch to school just like every other day but, unlike other days, I casually dropped it in the rubbish bin at the school gate. Yes, I know, millions of starving kids in Africa and all that, but that's what I did.

The morning dragged on, but I amused myself in History by making Mr Toppler, a doddery old thing on the edge of perpetual befuddlement, pick up a piece of chalk and put it down again without writing anything on the blackboard.

I managed to get him to pick up and put down the chalk over thirteen times before the bell rang for lunchtime.

Old Mr Toppler was easy. I think I could have made him eat the chalk if I had wanted to.

Mrs Mandible, the bad-tempered lizard, who ran the school tuck shop, was altogether a different story.

The air was moist with almost-rain as I made my way to the shop in the basement of the library. It faced the old D and E blocks and was at the end of a long covered walkway.

E Block and the Library joined together at the corner in a strange little wind trap. Every time the wind blew from the south, which was often, it would create whirlwinds in the corner. There was one of those today, a miniature tornado that picked up old leaves and bits of rubbish and spun them around and around before spitting them out again.

There was a sudden heavy shower as I waited in the queue, and I was grateful for the covered walkway. I was amazed at how many kids bought their lunch. Didn't their parents know about numbers?

The closer I got to the end of the line, the more nervous I got. It had seemed so simple in the planning, but to actually go through with it was something else again. A sudden blustery fist of rain punched in under the cover and I wiped cold droplets off my face. Maybe this wasn't such a good idea.

There was a line on the concrete floor that marked the start of the lower courtyard and it seemed like a barrier. Once I was past that line I would be inside the metal barriers of the tuck-shop queue. After that point, there would be no turning back. The more I looked at it, the more that line seemed to separate my quite ordinary and uneventful life, from my new life of crime. If I was going to back out, it had to be now. But there was a sudden surge in the queue and I was across the line and into the barriers.

I had passed the point of no return.

A few moments later, I was face to face with Mrs Mandible. She scowled at me over a box of flavoured noodle packets, and I almost lost my nerve once again.

But not quite.

'Potato-top pie and a cream donut,' I said casually, as if I ate such food every day. As if I robbed the school tuck shop every day.

Mandible snarled the price, and I held up a ten dollar note but, as she moved to take it, said, 'Oh, sorry, and a vanilla Coke.'

She scowled as if I had just stood on her tail but turned to the fridge for the drink. The moment her back was turned, I tucked the ten dollar note into the top pocket of my shirt, out of sight.

Mandible turned back. 'Is that all?'

He already paid me. He already paid me. He already paid

me. I painted pictures on her brain but said only, 'Yes, thank you, Mrs Mandible.'

She seemed a little confused and looked around for the money.

He already paid me. He already paid me. He already paid me.

'Did you, er . . .' She was a little flustered. Not like her at all.

'I already paid you,' I said confidently.

'Of course you did. Ten dollars right?'

I just nodded, but my knees were pressed together tightly with excitement. It was going to work.

Mrs Mandible counted out my change quickly and dismissed me with a shake of her head, snaring the next kid in line with her reptilian gaze.

I picked up my ill-gotten gains, pocketed my loot and turned to go. It was the perfect crime. Simple, quick, profitable and no-one was hurt (unless you counted the lizard lady).

I turned just in time to see Jason Kirk, another year nine kid, go sprawling across the wet concrete of the courtyard.

I guess he was hurrying to the lunch queue because of the rain, or maybe he just tripped. He was something of a klutz, Jason, and was always tripping over or dropping stuff. Some people said Jason was a bit slow, because of the way he talked and the weird way he wrote stuff. I didn't know him very well, but the couple of times I had talked to him he had seemed pretty switched on. He spoke slowly, but there was a bright spark in his conversation. As I said, though, I didn't know him very well. He wasn't in my class and hung out mainly with Daniel Taylor the rugby league star.

Jason hit the ground hard, and skidded a bit across the wet concrete. Something brown skittered out of his hand and disappeared through the grate of one of the storm water drains just in front of him.

I wondered what it was. It was only when he hauled himself to his feet and crouched by the drain, poking and peering down between the bars that I realized it was his lunch money, sealed up in a plain brown envelope by his mother, with a list of what he wanted and a sum of the prices. I had seen him with similar envelopes before.

The rain was heavy now, and blood was running down one of his legs from a skinned knee, but he crouched by the drain. It was futile, I thought. Those drains were deep, and if there were coins in the envelope it would have gone straight to the bottom.

I felt a bit sorry for him, but not that sorry. Things like that happened to me, and nobody ever gave a stuff.

But then someone in the lunch queue laughed.

Suddenly, someone did give a stuff. Me. It was bad enough getting wet, skinning his knee and missing out on lunch, without other kids laughing at him.

I walked over, hunched against the heavy shower and trying to shield my hot meat pie from the rain.

He looked up as I approached and cringed a little as if he thought I was going to attack him. His face was doing that funny thing kids do when they want to cry like a little boy, but know they can't, because they're at high school now.

I could see the end of the envelope sticking up out of the water at the bottom of the drain, but, even as I watched, the current swirled it away.

'Bad luck,' I said.

'Wouldn't that make your bum spit monkeys,' Jason agreed, trying to smile against the threatening tears. It seemed a strange thing to say, but I kinda knew what he meant.

I stretched out a hand to help him to his feet and, to my surprise, he accepted it. I wouldn't have, if it had been me.

'Thanks . . . um . . . Jacob,' he said, still peering forlornly down at the drain as if the current might miraculously bring his lunch money back and spit it up through the grill. It was a testament to how well I managed to keep to myself that most of the kids at school didn't even know my name. Jason did though.

I let go of his hand, and he looked up in surprise at the coins there.

'Godzilla in the tuck shop over-changed me,' I said, and it was almost true, in a way. 'Easy come, easy go. You have it.'

'I couldn't . . .' Jason began, but I was already walking away. I had somehow ended up with one friend at this school. The last thing I needed was another.

It was a funny feeling walking away through the rain, still trying to keep my pie dry. I had just pulled off my first crime. I was on the career path of a super-criminal. And yet first chance I'd had, I'd given away some of my loot.

I suppose I felt a bit like Robin Hood. Stealing from the rich (Mrs Mandible) and giving to the poor (wet bleeding hungry Jason Kirk).

I looked back and saw Jason joining the end of the lunch queue, his hands clenched tightly around the money. But then I saw another set of eyes, and that Robin Hood feeling vanished.

Erica McDonald had seen the whole thing. I could tell by her face that she thought I was some kind of hero.

Except I didn't feel like a hero. I didn't even feel like a super-villain.

Under her warm gaze, I felt like a bit of a fraud. Like a common criminal. Like the Hunchback Robber.

'Wouldn't that just make your bum spit monkeys,' I muttered to myself and hurried off through the rain.

12

Super Freak

Friday came all too quickly and the long cold windows of the old hall frowned disapprovingly at me as I dragged my feet along the path after last period.

I could hear laughter and chatter from inside the hall, and all around me kids were hurrying along.

News of the big fight had spread far and wide, and it seemed like the whole school was coming along to see Blocker bash the living crap out of the freak. Me.

I was sort of hoping that one of the teachers might have heard about it and would shut it down. But that would only postpone it, or worse, lead to a beating on the way home. And in any case, the kids kept things like this pretty quiet.

Ben was walking next to me, not saying anything, but instinctively supporting me anyway. That helped. At least I didn't feel quite so alone.

My only hope was to use my power to somehow control Blocker during the fight. Maybe I could convince him that I was a martial arts expert and make him nervous. Or maybe I could . . . well, actually, I didn't really hold out much hope. Still I had to try.

Blocker was in his gym gear already, bouncing around in the ring, shadow boxing some imaginary opponent.

'Hope you brought your undertaker with you!' he jeered as I entered. The crowd was swelling around the ring. I acted confident and brave, as if I expected to win the fight. But I think the crowd saw through that in a second.

I got changed quickly. No sense in getting my uniform torn. Mum couldn't afford to buy me another one.

Blocker was wearing cool Nike shorts and a sleeveless tank-top with a silver fern on it. My gym gear was just an old white pair of shorts and t-shirt.

Blocker smirked as I climbed under the ropes into the ring.

'Two rounds, three minutes each,' Phil Domane called importantly, acting as the ringmaster. There was no referee. No need I suppose. There were no rules. 'In the blue shorts, our reigning champion, Blocker! And in the funny white pants . . .' the crowd roared with laughter, '. . .our challenger . . .'

Phil turned and sneered at me. 'What's your nickname, Freak?'

I stared him down while I thought about it. I was no ordinary freak. I had a super-power! The name just came to me out of nowhere. 'Call me Super Freak.'

That threw him for a moment. I guess it wasn't so much fun calling me a freak if I called myself that too. Somehow I felt I had gained a small victory. He repeated the name to the crowd, and there was more laughter, but mixed in with it was a smattering of applause.

Well, they rang the bell and all hell broke loose. Blocker jumped up out of his corner and rushed at me, I didn't even have time to formulate a thought of my own, let alone try and influence Blocker. I ducked as best as I could beneath his outstretched arm but, even so, it caught me a glancing blow across the top of my head. It knocked me over backwards and made me see stars.

I tried to scramble to my feet, but Blocker was already on me, dive-bombing me before I could even move, a giant body slam right across my stomach that knocked all the air out of my lungs.

Blocker rolled away, and, somehow, I got back to my feet, winded and gasping for breath, leaning on the ropes for support.

He grinned at me from the other side of the ring, but made the mistake of trying the same thing again.

I wasn't much of a fighter but I wasn't stupid.

This time as he rushed at me, I stuck my hands up as if to fight him but, really, only to distract him and, just at the last moment, I stepped to one side and stuck out my foot.

He tripped and went skidding across the ring, banging his head good and proper on the corner post.

When he got up, there was a trickle of blood running down his forehead and the look in his eyes had turned from one of amusement to one of rage.

I focused on his brain and thought furiously, *the Freak knows karate, he's going to beat you, he knows karate, he's going to beat you.*

I guess I was trying to put him off, and there was a momentary hesitation and a look of uncertainty on Blocker's face. But only for a second, then it was gone and Blocker was on me once again, grabbing me around the waist and pile-driving me into the canvas floor of the ring.

I came up spitting blood and fearing for my life.

He knows karate, he's going to beat you, he knows . . .

It had no effect on the enraged bull that was Blocker. He slammed me on to my back on the canvas and dropped on top of me again, driving an elbow into my ribs.

I though I heard something crack and a ferocious pain stabbed across my chest.

I had barely got back to my feet when a vicious arm that I never even saw coming smashed into my face, and, this time when I got up, blood was pouring from my nose.

In the midst of it all, the only good thing running through my brain was that at least I wasn't crying.

Blocker came in once again, circling for the kill but, somehow, I was ready for him, and darted to one side. I charlied him in the thigh and Blocker went down for the second time. This time when he got up, limping, there was murder in his eyes.

I backed away into the side of the ring as he approached, slowly this time, and suddenly found myself flat on my back on the canvas again as he swept my legs out from underneath me with his foot.

I coughed, splattering the front of his expensive gym shirt with blood, and he drew his fist back and smashed it into my face.

Now, I was crying, and couldn't help myself, but something told me that this was only the start.

There was a strange murmuring in the crowd but I couldn't see what was happening.

I wondered if a teacher might have walked in and would stop it. But another voice in my brain said, if that did happen, somehow it would be Jacob the trouble-maker who ended up in trouble, and not Blocker, the school hero.

Blocker drew his fist back once again and struck, but this

time the punch didn't connect. I had instinctively closed my eyes and opened them to see Blocker's arm caught in a vice.

A vice that was the hand of a boy named Tupai White.

I couldn't make sense of it at first. In fact, I didn't make sense of it till later, but I suppose my brain was a little addled at the time.

Blocker stood up and turned to face Tupai, his wrist still jammed in the steel-mesh grip of Tupai's hand.

'It's not your fight,' he snarled, but, even as he said it, he punched hard and straight at Tupai's stomach. The punch never made it. It stopped half way there, his other wrist snared in Tupai's free hand.

Blocker clenched and muscled up, trying to break Tupai's grip. Tupai hardly even seemed to be trying. Slowly, he lifted Blocker's wrists into the air above his head. It was a terrific feat of strength. He twisted Blocker around and pulled the wrists down again behind Blocker's back, pinning him.

'Leave him alone,' Tupai said and repeated it. 'Leave him alone. Here, at school, after school, if you touch him again, you'll be talking to me.'

I saw Erica McDonald standing at the side of the ring, looking on, and even that didn't connect for quite a while afterwards.

'He challenged me!' Blocker protested, but Tupai was not having any of that.

'Touch him again, and you are mincemeat. Am I clear?'

Blocker looked around, trying to summon some courage. He might have been big and tough but, compared to Tupai, he was a snowflake. Tupai, at thirteen, was probably the toughest kid in the whole school, and not even the Year

Twelves or Thirteens were game to take him on.

Not that Tupai went looking for fights. Quite the opposite. But they sometimes found him and, when they did, the other party always ended up sorry for it.

But just why he would jump in the ring and stick up for me made no sense. I looked at Erica, and she gave me a kind of a half smile, but then turned quickly and was gone. Tupai went with her. Ben jumped in the ring and helped me to my feet, wiping away blood from my face with his own shirt, never minding the mess.

Blocker half-moved towards me, but his eyes were on Tupai's retreating back, and there was genuine fear there. I suspected that, like most bullies, underneath he was a coward.

It was finally over. I cleaned myself up in the showers as best as I could and changed back into my uniform. One of my eyes was so swollen I could hardly see out of it, but at least my nose had stopped bleeding.

On the way home I finally put it all together. Tupai White and Jason Kirk were best mates, along with Daniel the league-player and another guy called Fizzy, or Fizzer, something like that.

Erica had seen what I had done for Jason at the tuck shop and she must have told Tupai what was going on.

Tupai had stood up for me because I had stood up for his mate. It shook me a little, when I realized. The trails of their friendship ran deep.

However, I wasn't sure if he had really done me a favour. If he hadn't stepped in, then at least it would have been all over and done with in the boxing ring.

Now, even under the protective wing of Tupai, I felt that Blocker would not just give up and go away.

Whatever was churning inside him would be growing more malignant by the hour.

13

Crikey!

'Crikey!' Mum took one look at me and borrowed the neighbour's car to take me to the hospital. I really didn't feel too bad, apart from the pain in my chest, but I guess I must have looked quite frightening.

Ben had walked home with me and carried my schoolbag because, when I tried to lift it, the stabbing sensation in my chest became a burning twisting knife.

Dad was out at an audition for a commercial and couldn't be reached on his mobile, so Mum went next door and explained to Mrs McLatcheon, who was a kindly old soul, that there was an emergency and asked if she could borrow her Morris Minor. Ben came to Outpatients with us, which was good of him, and Gumbo refused to be left behind. (Although he had to stay in the car, whining madly, when we got to the hospital.)

It was just cuts and bruises, the doctor assured us, no broken bones. The rib thing turned out to be a cartilage, and would heal all by itself given enough time.

I had told Mum that I had fallen off the jungle gym at

school, and I think she believed me, but Dad didn't. He was already home from his audition by the time we got back.

'How's the other guy?' he asked conspiratorially when Mum was out of the room.

I looked at him closely for a while, wondering how much to tell him. Eventually, with a quick glance at Ben, I just said, 'He won't be bothering me any more.' Which was true, I suppose.

'Good on ya,' Dad winked at me. 'You show them who's who.'

I think he was quite proud of me, and I couldn't be bothered to set him right.

Ben waited till my dad was out of the room, then whispered in amazement, 'Your dad's that policeman from the dog-food commercial!'

14

The Student Council

Quite a few things happened the next week which are all worth mentioning. The first excitement was Dad being invited to audition for a role on *Shortland Street*. The job was an initial ten week stint as a new Russian doctor. Dad assured us the role would almost certainly become a part of the core cast. A regular.

The very thought of it made unforeseen riches dance in front of our eyes. Imagine what life would be like if Dad had a permanent and well-paid job. A cast-regular on a soapie like *Shortland Street* pulled in as much as a highly-paid businessman. There'd be new clothes. A car for sure, and maybe Mum and Dad would even be able to save up enough money for a deposit on a house.

A house of our own.

The excitement level was almost at fever pitch, despite the fact that Dad's audition was still two or three weeks away.

Funnily enough, this small glimpse of what we were missing made me more determined than ever to become the greatest criminal mastermind this country has ever seen. I wanted money. I wanted nice things like other kids. But, most of all, I wanted to be in charge of my own life, not to be at the whim and will of everyone around me.

I had a good evil villain name. I was *Super Freak*. Even Batman would be glad to battle an enemy with a name like that. But what I needed was a super-crime, and that opportunity was handed to me on a plate the next week at school.

The other thing that happened was that I somehow summonsed up the courage, or the stupidity, to ask Erica out. Well, to be totally honest, I was blackmailed into it.

And yet another thing, which wasn't at all good, was that I started getting text messages from Blocker on my mobile phone.

It all started on the Saturday, I guess. On the Friday night I had brought home a school newsletter which was partly about the election of a student council (a bit late if you asked me, with the year half over) but mostly about the announcement of the upcoming Spring School Fair. They'd given it a title, *Spring Fever,* which I thought was a bit naff, but it didn't worry me because it gave me an idea for my super-crime. My *Crime of the Century.*

I spent the whole morning thinking about it and starting to make plans. The annual school fair raised thousands of dollars each year for the school. Tens of thousands of dollars. All of it in small, untraceable bills. More money than I'd seen in my life! And on the Saturday of the school fair it would all be held somewhere on the school grounds, while they counted and sorted it. All I had to do was find out where and figure out a way to get my hands on it.

It wouldn't be easy, but it wouldn't be a super-crime if it was easy. It was just the task for *Super Freak* with his awesome super-powers. Well, super-power, if you want to be pedantic about it.

The student council was going to help organize the school fair this year. The kids on the council would know what was going on, where the money was, everything. So, I had to get an insider on the student council, and I knew it wouldn't be me, the trouble-maker.

Ben came around in the afternoon to watch the Warriors playing against the Machetes at the Blacktown Stadium in Sydney. The Machetes were top-of-the-table in the competition so far, but the Warriors were in second place and snapping at their heels.

Ben didn't have a television in his house. Apparently his parents didn't believe in it. They also weren't too keen on rugby or rugby league, so Ben was being a bit of a rebel when he came over to my place.

The weather had cleared up a bit after the last few wet weekends, in fact it was pouring sun over the place as if it were a summer's day, not mid-winter, and Mum was out in the garden pulling some weeds. She greeted Ben at the front gate with a cheery, 'G'day mate.'

She had a cold beer sitting in the milk-compartment of the rusty old letterbox, and she stopped working for a minute and wiped her brow with the can before taking a long drink.

She's a bit of a farm-girl, my mum, which is odd as her dad was an accountant in Nelson, and she grew up in the town centre, not out in the country. She calls everybody 'mate', and likes the occasional beer. She doesn't go in for fancy clothes or expensive hair-dos and, in many ways, is exactly the opposite of Dad, who spends a lot of time, and what little money we have, on the right clothes, the latest mobile phone, and keeping himself groomed. It is important for his job, he often explains.

Dad was in the garage working on an old chesterfield with a broken leg. I hoped he would stay there. He was busy preparing himself for the upcoming audition, which meant immersing himself totally in the character. He was stomping around the house talking to everyone in a thick Russian accent and answering questions with *Da* and *Nyet*, instead of *Yes* and *No*.

It had become a bit of a ritual for Ben to come over and watch the Warriors with me and Gumbo. And it was always the same. We watched, we cheered, we held our breath when we saw Daniel warming up on the sideline, but the ending never changed. Daniel stayed on the reserves' bench and didn't take part in the game.

This was an exciting game, so it took a while before there was a quiet patch and I could ask Ben the big question.

'Have you thought about running for the student council?' I asked casually as if it were the most natural thing in the world.

He looked sideways at me, raising his eyebrows in a slow mechanical manner. 'Me?'

'Why not?'

'That's for the popular kids. I wouldn't get a look in.'

He was right, of course, but I thought I could swing that part of it if I could get him to step forward.

'I'd nominate you, and I reckon most of the class would vote you in,' I said.

'You're nuts,' he said and turned back to the game, where a big Warrior named Henry Knight was busting a huge hole in the Machetes' line.

The student council was to be formed by one representative from each class, and I desperately wanted Ben to be the rep for our class.

I suggested carefully, 'You might be surprised at how many people vote for you.'

He shook his head without speaking and concentrated on the game.

Gumbo was lying half on the sofa, half flopped across Ben's lap, and Ben tousled the big dog's ears absent-mindedly. If dogs could purr, Gumbo would have purred just then.

Dad came into the room, a chisel in his hand.

'Vos is dis geem?' he said in his mangled Russian. 'Ees dees de Varriors?'

'Da,' said Ben automatically, and I cracked up laughing.

Dad nodded seriously. 'Pleez to be letting me know who vinning de geem ees.'

'Warriors are in front at the moment,' I said quickly, wanting to get rid of him so I could get on with talking Ben into running for the council.

'Da. Gud, gud,' and with that he disappeared into the kitchen, searching for something in the cupboards.

Just at that moment, the big guy, Henry, burst right through the Machetes' defences and dropped over the line for a try.

The crowd roared. Ben and I shouted and leapt off the couch. Gumbo leapt up also, barking furiously at the screen.

'Gumbo's a real Warriors' fan, isn't he?' Ben said, as Ainsley Retimanu, the Warriors' first five-eights, slotted the ball between the posts for the conversion. 'Do you think he knows what's going on?'

I laughed. 'I reckon he's right up with it. Dad took me and Gumbo to a game once – Daniel's first game, in fact, against the Machetes – at Ericsson stadium, and he barked every time we got the ball.'

Ben looked a bit doubtful. 'Really? But how did you smuggle a dog into the stadium?'

'Dad put on a pair of dark glasses and told them that Gumbo was his seeing-eye dog. He's a pretty good actor, my dad, and he had them all convinced that he was really blind.'

Ben laughed.

I continued. 'It all went well until Rumble Bean stiff-armed Bazza, knocking him out cold. It should have been a penalty, but neither the ref, nor the linesmen did anything. Dad jumped to his feet, forgetting all about his dark glasses, and shouted out, "What's the matter with you, Ref, are you blind!" Everyone around us was staring at him.'

Ben doubled over with laughter, and Gumbo gave a series of funny snorts. He was smarter than he looked, that dog.

'But, worse, just then the camera picked him up and put him on the big screen.'

Ben finally stopped laughing long enough to say, 'Just as well you two aren't at the game today.'

'Why?'

'Vots de mata wiv you, Rev, blind ees you?' Ben shrieked in a perfect imitation of Dad's Russian accent.

I missed the next two minutes of the game, I was laughing so hard.

'Vot abote you, Gumby?' Ben called out to the dog. 'You zink ze Vorriers es goink to vin?'

'Da,' Gumbo barked, clear as day, and that set us off again.

A few minutes later we weren't laughing quite so loud. Henry Knight had been hurt in a vicious tackle by Rumble Bean and had to be stretchered off the field. He was a good and popular player, and we felt quite badly about it.

'Bean should have been sent off for that,' Ben muttered.

There was a silver lining to the dark cloud, though. A few moments later, after countless games sitting on the bench, Daniel Taylor finally took the field for the Warriors. Their youngest player, by far, to ever play in a first grade match.

It seemed to take an age before he even got to touch the ball but, when he did, it was like a flash of light, and somehow he was down the end of the field scoring a try.

'He's fantastic!' Ben said.

'He's brilliant!' I added.

'Da!' Gumbo agreed.

The game finished. We won. When we finally calmed down from all the excitement, I tackled Ben again about the student council.

'No way,' he said. 'No one would vote for me, and I'd be totally humiliated.'

I guess I could have used my special power to try and change his mind. But it felt wrong, doing that to a friend. So, I just said, 'No you wouldn't.'

'Yes, I would.'

'Well, what's wrong with a little humiliation?'

Ben looked at me strangely. 'So why haven't you asked Erica McDonald out?'

I jerked upright and stared at him. 'What are you talking about?'

He said, 'She's gorgeous, and you make Gumbo eyes at her every time she walks past. So why haven't you asked her out?'

I stared blankly at him. 'Because she'd laugh at me, and I'd be totally humiliated.'

'Hmmm . . .' said Ben, meaningfully.

'It's not the same.'

'It's exactly the same.'

We stared at each other for a while, then Ben said, 'OK, I'll do you a deal. You ask Erica out on a date, and I'll run for student council. That way we'll both get totally humiliated and it'll be even.'

I started to say no, but then thought about it and realized that it was a sacrifice I would have to make if I wanted to be a master criminal. After all, the pain and humiliation would not last long.

'You have to ask her properly,' Ben said. 'Not just mutter it in passing, in the corridor.'

'Yeah, and you have to really try to get on the student council.'

'OK, deal.'

'Deal.'

And that was it. It was done.

15

Erica McGorgeous

I tried twice to ask Erica out before I actually did it. On the Monday, I nominated Ben for the student council and there was a bit of a snigger from the back of the room, but we both ignored it.

Speeches were to be on the Thursday, after which there would be a vote and our class representative would be elected.

I spent most of the week, whenever I had the chance, brainwashing the other members of our class into voting for Ben Holly.

I sat behind Matthew Clay in Geography and spent the entire lesson sending his brain messages that Ben Holly would be a good class representative.

I did the same in History to the Butler twins and followed Chelsie Burnett down the corridors of C Block thinking *Vote for Ben Holly* as hard as I could. I would have reached out to most of the class in one way or another during those couple of days but I knew for certain it would all be to no avail if Ben withdrew on the Thursday.

He was threatening to do it, too – every day that I didn't

get around to my end of the bargain. Asking out gorgeous Erica McDonald.

I managed to walk out of French with Erica on Tuesday morning (one of the few classes we shared) and we were side by side going down the stairs. It was the perfect opportunity, but I glanced across at her just as I was about to open my mouth and completely lost my nerve.

The problem was I didn't want to hear her say no. Ben was right. I was all Gumbo-eyed about her and, as long as I didn't ask her and she didn't say 'no', then there was still the chance, however tiny, that she might want to go out with me. But, as soon as I asked the question, then the truth would come out and the humiliation would begin.

It's funny how we would rather hear no answer at all than hear the answer we don't want.

My second chance was at lunch the same day. Erica was sitting by herself on a bench in the concrete desert that was the D-Block quad. Alone. Aloof. Living in her own world, isolated from the frenzied lunchtime goings-on around her.

I stood for a while, gathering my courage, and finally started to march across the quad towards her.

Halfway there, my mobile beeped with a text message.

I stopped and checked my message.

I didn't know the number, but it wasn't hard to work out the sender.

GONNA GETCHA FREAK, it spelled out.

I took a deep breath and thrust the phone back in my pocket. Blocker's latest game. Still, he didn't dare touch me, so it was just empty threats.

Before I had taken another step, my phone beeped again. GONNA GETCHA GOOD, was the new message.

I tried to shrug it off again but I was quite rattled now. I looked over at Erica, still eating her lunch on the lonely bench. *Another day,* I said to myself, and hurried off to find Ben.

Ben thought I should report the texts to the principal or show them to Tupai, but I didn't want to do either. I felt both would just make matters worse. Ben ribbed me a bit for chickening out of talking to Erica and reminded me there were just two days to go. He wasn't too tough on me though. He could tell I was a bit thrown, by the text messages I mean.

Wednesday was a big day at school. There was a home game of rugby league scheduled for just after lunch, and it was a big event. For a start, it was against Birkenhead College, our arch-rivals in the under-fifteens, and it was a semi-final to decide which team would meet Takapuna Grammar in the final. On top of this, the national schoolboy rugby league selectors would be there, judging performances and selecting trialists for the national under-fifteen squad which would be touring Australia later in the year. Both Phil and Blocker were playing.

The whole school turned out to watch, juniors and seniors alike. Even those who weren't the slightest bit interested in rugby league. All classes were cancelled for the game, and attendance was compulsory.

I thought I would engineer things so that I just happened to be sitting next to Erica during the game, but the grassy banks around the top rugby field were packed with students from our school and supporters from Birkenhead, who arrived by the bus-load, and I couldn't see Erica anywhere.

The game started with an explosion as Phil fed the ball to a wiry centre-half named McAlpine who passed it quickly to

Blocker as two massive Birkenhead forwards were about to monster him. Blocker dodged around his marker, with surprising agility for someone of his bulk, and found himself in a bit of space. Enough to get up a full head of steam.

Opposition players quickly closed up in front of him, but Blocker's speed was up now and he charged straight at them, aiming for the middle guy.

Bam! There was a thundering crash of bodies that we could hear from the banks, and Blocker exploded through the three of them, the outside two spinning off to either side, and the poor middle guy just going down backwards and getting trampled by the runaway bull that Blocker had become.

And there he was, Blocker the forward, Blocker the hero, charging at the line with only the fullback to beat. Their winger was giving chase from the other side but he wasn't going to get there in time.

McAlpine streaked up on the inside and called for the ball.

Pass the ball Blocker I thought, although I wasn't using my special power. I wasn't concentrating on Blocker's head.

Blocker hurtled towards the fullback, who didn't have a chance and, from the expression on his face, clearly knew it. The try was Blocker's. Then, just before the fullback leaped up for the tackle, Blocker unselfishly flipped the ball to McAlpine.

The fullback got brushed aside like an annoying insect, and Blocker shadowed McAlpine down to the try-line.

It should have been the perfect start to the game. An exciting and spectacular try. A try that Blocker could easily have scored himself, but handed the glory off to his team-mate. But McAlpine, instead of diving over the line or placing the ball carefully on the grass, went for a fancy one-handed put-down, undoubtedly trying to show off in front of the selectors, and he dropped the ball. He bombed the try, then tripped trying to recover the ball and ended up in a heap on the grass.

'Knock on,' the referee called.

Blocker ran over to McAlpine, the kid who had just butchered Blocker's certain try and cost us a good head start against Birkenhead. I expected him to be swearing and shouting. I almost expected him to thump him. But he didn't.

Blocker extended a hand, helping McAlpine to his feet, then patted him on the back and muttered a few words of encouragement, before trotting back to get ready for the resulting scrum.

'Good one, Blocker,' I muttered, but my feelings were more than a little mixed.

Somehow the rest of Wednesday slipped by and I knew that the next morning Ben was going to excuse himself from the elections and all would be lost. I was starting to get a bit desperate when, after school, I saw Erica walking home. She went a different way to me, but it wasn't too far from my route, so I traipsed along after her like a puppy dog following its master, feeling a bit pathetic.

It took about half a kilometre before I overcame my nerves, steeled myself for the inevitable outcome and quickened my pace so that I caught up with her.

She half-turned her head as I walked up alongside her but said nothing.

'Hi,' I said.

'Hello,' she said, without looking at me.

'I was wondering,' I started, and then couldn't get the rest of the words out.

'What?' she asked.

'If . . .' *Jeez this was hard.* 'If you . . . were planning on standing for the student council.'

What an idiot!

This time she did look at me, as if she thought I was quite strange. 'No. I'm not standing.'

'Oh.'

Ten steps, I thought. *I'll take ten more steps and then I'll ask her.*

Ten steps went by.

Just ten more steps. Ten, nine, eight . . . oh this is stupid.

'And I was wondering if you'd maybe, want to, like, maybe, you know, go out with me?'

There! I said it.

Silence.

'To a movie or something?'

Silence.

'Or not.'

She half glanced at me, and I could have sworn there were tears in her eyes, and then she was hurrying off, leaving me standing there on the grass verge of someone's driveway feeling very stupid and more confused than I'd ever been in my life.

'Well, at least I did it,' I said out loud to nobody and started to walk home.

16

The Election

I didn't feel quite so bad the next morning as I did the night before. I had lain awake, for half the night it seemed, just feeling stupid and sad and angry all at once. I wasn't even sure what I was angry about or who with. But things seemed clearer in the morning.

Sometime during the night, I'd also figured out my plan for stealing the proceeds of the Spring Fever Fair. I wasn't sure of the details; they would have to wait until I got some inside information from the school council. And that would depend on Ben winning the election.

But I did know one thing for sure. I was going to need some seed money. In order to pull off my plan I was going to need about fifty or sixty dollars cash. But I didn't have that kind of money, which meant another smaller crime to start with.

My career as a criminal was beginning to take shape. Super Freak versus the world!

The speeches were to start at 9 o'clock, so when the clock ticked around and Ben still hadn't arrived, I started to worry. Not for long, though, as he showed up a couple of moments later and mumbled an apology to the teacher, Mr Hawthorne, as he found his seat.

Luckily Erica wasn't in our home class. I wasn't sure I could have faced her that morning.

'I did it,' I told Ben in a whisper, forcing the words through a strange ache in my chest. 'I asked her out.'

'I know,' he whispered back. 'I saw her at the front gate. She gave me this.'

My heart pounded for no obvious reason as he passed me a small yellow envelope. A letter. *She had written me a letter!*

I was tingly, excited, and sorely tempted to open it and read it right away, but the speeches were starting. I saw Hawthorne looking at me.

If Hawthorne saw you passing notes, he would take them and read them aloud to the class. I had no idea of what was in the letter but, whatever it was, I knew I did *not* want it read out to my classmates.

I tucked the letter safely away and listened to the first speaker.

It was Jenny Kreisler. She was a popular girl, and I thought she'd probably win the election, if I couldn't swing it Ben's way with my special power.

She was supposed to be going out with Daniel Taylor, the league player, but I wasn't sure if that was true. He was never around anyway. He was always off at training or something.

She spoke well and persuasively, a succinct two minute speech in which she told us all about her abilities as a communicator and an organizer, and why she'd be good as a member of the student council. She was very good, so I thought this could be an even closer battle than I had anticipated.

Johnny Howard was next. He was a lean muscled boy, who

could sprint like the wind, and was the number eleven on the school year nine rugby team. He too spoke of his skills, his ability to relate to other people and see their point of view.

The next speaker, Sandra Greathouse, seemed to have borrowed Johnny's script notes, as she said almost the same things, but not as well, nervously staring at her palm-sized note-cards the whole time. I didn't rate her very well at all.

And on it went through a succession of speakers, eight in all, every one of them telling us how wonderful they were, what wonderful skills they had, and why they'd make a great student councillor. Until we got to the last speaker, Ben Holly.

He got slowly to his feet, and moved, with that robotic gait of his, to the front of the class.

He stood there for a while, looking around at us all but not saying anything. He had no speech cards at all.

I suddenly got worried. What if he made a real crap-fest of this? What if he really blew it? No amount of mental thought bending was going to get him elected if he totally bummed out in the election speeches.

He spoke then, and his voice lost its usual mechanical quality, sounding clear and confident throughout the room.

'I've heard you all speak,' he said, nodding to the other nominees, 'and all I can say is that I'd vote for each and every one of you. I think any of you would be great.'

What was he doing?!

'Jenny, you are a good communicator and a great organizer. Johnny, I know what you mean about relating to people, it is a rare gift you have to be able to do that. As for myself, I'm not so sure. I don't really know how I'd go on the school council, and I suspect that none of us really do for sure, until we find ourselves in that situation.'

He seemed to grow taller as he spoke, and there was a presence about him that took over and commanded the room.

'Have I got the right skills? I'd like to think so, but I'm not sure. But ask me if I have ideas, and the answer is yes!' He banged the desk in front of him for emphasis and a little jar of pens fell over, but no one even noticed.

'I've been thinking about what I'd do if I was elected, and I've got lots of ideas. I'd like to see more field trips for students. Give us a chance to see the real world in action. I'd like to see new tennis courts to replace those worn-out crater-pits down past the pre-fabs. I'd like to see a points-reward system for students who volunteer for activities around the school, with real prizes at the end of the year for those who collect most points. A school website with pages for each class to present news and show off examples of their work. I'd like to see . . .'

And on he went.

Whereas all the other kids had spent their two minutes telling us how great they were, Ben did none of that. He just told us all of his ideas for using the school council to stand up for student rights and to make the school a better place for students.

When the votes were tallied, Ben was the winner, beating Jenny Kreisler into second place by a clear margin.

I had blasted everyone in the room with a *choose Ben Holly* message when the voting started, but I don't think it had made any difference.

To my immense surprise, Ben Holly had won it on his own!

I ripped open the envelope the second the period bell sounded. It turned out to contain not a letter, but a short note.

Please meet me in the library after school on Friday.

Erica

That was all.

Friday seemed like an eternity away. Would it turn out to be a good thing or a bad thing? I had no idea.

17

The Old Stump

I walked home with Ben as usual on Thursday after school. We always took the same way. I was trying not to think about Erica, so I concentrated instead on the mechanical sound that Ben made when he moved.

Through the short concrete path, overgrown with thistles, leading to Acorn Park. Step ssshhh, step ssshhh. Along the side of Mr Dover's house. He was always at home limping around the garden, while his wife was out at work. Step ssshhh, step ssshhh. Past the old stump which all the kids avoided because it had a huge nest of nasty-tempered wasps inside. Step ssshhh, step ssshhh, step ssshhh.

I was just about past the stump when I saw Blocker and Phil Domane standing amongst the massive oak trees of the park, half hidden from view, and I instinctively knew what they were going to do.

'Run!' I shouted, and Ben, although he hadn't seen them, obeyed automatically. We sprinted into the park away from the danger.

I saw the blur of Blocker's arm. The rock that he chucked – on reflection I think it was a broken-off chunk of concrete –

94

seemed to hang in the air almost indefinitely as it flew towards the nest in the old stump.

Mr Dover was out watering his garden and he glanced up, his eye caught by the movement. I looked back and saw Caitlin Howard, Johnny Howard's little sister, enter the other end of the concrete path. She was six-years-old I think, still young enough to let her mum put her hair in pigtails, and she went to a nearby primary school. Usually she walked home with her big brother. Not today though, he must have had sports practice.

I caught my breath, unsure of what to do. Somehow, behind me, I was aware that Ben had also stopped and turned back to face the impending disaster.

Caitlin walked. The rock flew. Mr Dover watered. I froze.

The rock smashed into the stump with a muffled woody thump and cracked off, rolling over the grass to end up against Mr Dover's back fence.

The wasps' nest exploded into a hurricane of hurtling furious yellow and black shapes, writhing around the stump. I involuntarily took a couple of quick steps backwards, even though I was well clear of the danger zone. The cloud around the stump spread, seeking targets, but not moving too far from the nest it was defending.

Mr Dover was looking at the stump with a horrified glare and walking backwards as fast as he could, the hose in his hand spraying uselessly over his lawn.

Little Caitlin Howard kept on walking. Her head was down. She was lost in some private world, oblivious to the escalating whine of the swarming wasps.

As she neared the end of the path I heard someone shouting, 'Caitlin, go back! Caitlin, go back!' and realized with surprise it was me.

It was too late by that stage, though, far too late. She looked up as she wondered what was wrong. The wasps were already buzzing all around her.

Any kid would surely have run back out of the danger, but she didn't. Maybe six-year-olds think differently or, more likely, when faced with such terror, she instinctively headed for a place of safety – home. The problem was her path home lay right through the seething cloud.

I watched, helplessly, as she took one tiny step after another, her arms waving frantically around her head. I am sure she screamed the first time she was stung, and maybe the second and third but, after that, it just became a long drawn-out wail, a single long breath until she was well past the stump. Thinking she was out of danger, or just unable to run any more, she dropped, hunched over, legs splayed on the grass, bawling. That was the second mistake she made and it was a bigger mistake than the first.

She was well within range of the nest and the wasps followed her, gathering in a cloud around her as she sat on the ground, stinging her again and again as she wailed and squealed in anguish.

Mr Dover had turned his hose on the nest. I think he thought that would help or maybe he just didn't know what else to do, but even I knew that it is smoke that calms down angry wasps, not water. Water makes them angrier. As he poured, more wasps came spraying up out of the nest.

Caitlin just sat there. I wanted to run up to her, to grab her and haul her out of there, but I couldn't – or maybe just wouldn't – move. I simply wasn't brave enough to run into a swarm of angry wasps. Phil and Blocker, like me, were frozen, horrified, petrified.

Without thinking, I looked back at Ben. The single bizarre thought in my mind was that he should go and save her. What did a few wasp stings matter to a robot anyway, even if they could sting through his rubberised robotic skin?

He looked back at me, right into my eyes, and it was as if he could tell what I was thinking. He took a few faltering steps forwards, dropped his schoolbag and then began to run.

Ben Holly, the new student councillor and my best friend, ran into the storm.

He didn't stop, he didn't change direction. He just scooped Caitlin roughly up by the arm and pulled her, dragging her away from the swarm, to the far corner of the park.

The wasps chased for a little while, and a few of the nastier ones followed for quite a long way, but they soon all retreated to their nest and resumed circling and threatening.

I hadn't seen Mr Dover disappear, but he was gone. Stupid fart. Maybe he'd been stung too. If so, he deserved it.

I circled around the park to where Caitlin was, giving the nest a wide berth. Her face was a red raw mass, and her arms and legs were already rising into a wilderness of pain.

'Where do you live?' Ben was asking, over and over.

She said nothing. Maybe she couldn't. Her eyes were waxy and she was leaning against his arm as if she couldn't hold herself upright. She had stopped crying, but I sensed it was a bad thing, not a good thing.

'I know where she lives.' It was Phil, behind me. 'I'll take her.' He looked at me and flinched, and I knew that my thoughts must have been reflected on my face. Blocker picked up her school bag, and Phil picked Caitlin up, carrying her in his arms like a baby. Then they set off at a half-run, with just one backwards, guilty glance.

Ben and I stayed where we were as they disappeared around the corner. I found I was staring at the raised welts on his neck and the back of his hands. He hardly seemed to notice.

We stayed there for a long time, watching the gradually diminishing swirls of wasps, before heading off home.

18

Assembly

The next day there was an assembly at school. Just an ordinary Friday assembly except that Mr Curtis, the principal, made special mention of the wasp attack.

'A little girl was seriously hurt,' he intoned down at us from his dais on the stage, like a minister in church. 'She's in the hospital but she's stable, and they think she's going to be OK.'

I breathed a sigh of relief at that and noticed that the other kids around me were unusually quiet for a Friday assembly.

Mr Curtis was tall and thin with the most atrocious comb-over I'd ever seen in my life. Even now, long grey wisps had escaped and were hanging down past his ear.

'Her mother has asked that the school thank the boys who saved her from the wasps, and the local community constable wants to nominate them for a special heroism medal.' Mr Curtis was enjoying this. I think he was proud that some of his pupils had become heroes. As if, somehow, that reflected on his guidance as the principal.

I looked behind me at Ben, sitting a few rows away. He looked back at me, but kept his face impassively, robotically, blank.

'Would the heroic boys who did this brave deed, please stand up.'

I looked back at Ben again, but he made no effort to move. Maybe he really was a robot, I thought. There was no emotion in his face at all.

There was a strange silence, and I was almost going to call out Ben's name, he deserved the recognition, even if he didn't want it for some strange, unknowable reason.

But I didn't. Then there was a noise in front of me and I looked around to see Phil and Blocker – the rock thrower – get to their feet. I sucked in my breath to stop myself from crying out. They had taken her home but they weren't the ones who rescued her!

'Good,' Curtis said pompously. 'Well done, lads. And you might also like to know that as a gesture of our sincere appreciation, the school, with a little help from the local Rotary club, has decided to make a gift of one hundred dollars to each of you as a reward for your actions.'

My mouth dropped open. The applause was spontaneous and seemed to go on forever.

19

The Navy Destroyer

We had PE that afternoon, and Old Sea Salt was in a particularly sadistic mood. Mrs Winters was away, so her class had been combined with Saltham's which meant that Tupai White, Daniel Taylor and Fraser (Fizzer) Boyd were among the others sharing the gym. Jason Kirk would have been there too, except he had sprained his ankle the previous day and had a pass.

I was trying to concentrate on the exercises, but my mind kept going to the library and my meeting with Erica after school. Why did she want to meet? What did she want? Would it be good or was I going to regret it?

'How are you doing?' Tupai asked me with a grin, as we found ourselves at the bottom of a rope-climbing exercise together.

I just nodded.

'Is he leaving you alone?' Tupai flicked a glance over at Blocker, leaning against a wall, talking to Phil.

'Yeah, it's cool.' I deliberately didn't tell Tupai about the text messages. I didn't want to make matters any worse than they already were.

Tupai started to say something else but Saltham shouted, 'Go!' and clicked a stopwatch hanging around his neck.

I grabbed my rope but by the time I was half way up, Tupai had already reached the ground again. He had just hauled himself up the rope on those powerful arms, scarcely bothering about his feet, except to steady himself. He'd reached the top, slapped the wooden beam to show he'd made it, and slid easily back down.

Saltham seemed quite startled. 'Good,' he said and made some notes on his clipboard. He made another note when I finally made it to the top and slapped the beam, but didn't say anything to me.

Blocker made even harder going of the rope exercise when it was his turn, which gave me a small inner smile of satisfaction. He was strong, but he had a lot of weight to haul up the rope. He was sweating like anything when he finally reached the top and just about slipped off the rope.

If he had fallen and broken his neck, would I have been sorry? Probably, but I couldn't say for certain.

The next exercise was a new one, and I looked on it with utter dread. I never seemed to be much good at these things. I knew if I failed, Saltham would just make me keep trying and trying until I got it right or got detention, which made me twice as nervous and half as likely to succeed.

The exercise went like this. Two helpers would stand in front of you and grasp each others' wrists. You had to run at them and do a kind of handstand in front of them, except that you would fall forward on to their joined arms and flip back over on to your feet again.

Then you would take the place of one of the helpers.

It sounds pretty straight-forward, and most of the kids had

no problem with it. They just ran into it, somersaulted through the air with the help of the other two guys, landed on their feet and went to take their place as a helper.

I ended up behind Fizzer Boyd. Tupai was in front of him.

Tupai sprang forward and vaulted over the outstretched arms easily, although there was a grunt from both of his helpers as they took the full brunt of his bulk. He took over from Stubby Forsyth.

Fizzer ran forward, and I swear I've never seen anything like it. He sprang into the handstand and flipped his body over the outstretched arms like an Olympic gymnast. The two helpers never touched him.

He landed cat-like on the other side and there was a spontaneous round of applause from the on-lookers. Fizzer smiled and made a small bow, before taking the place of Mike Pinkington.

I can do this. I thought. *I can do this*.

I ran forward, placed my hands on the ground in exactly the right place . . . and my arms collapsed. I tumbled into a forward roll, breaking Fizzer and Tupai's hands apart as my legs crashed through where my back ought to have been.

Fizzer rubbed his wrist, although Tupai didn't seem bothered.

'Sorry,' I muttered, wincing with embarrassment.

'Again!' Saltham called out from the far side of the hall.

Red-faced, I circled around back to the start. I stopped and took a deep breath.

I can do this.

I ran forward again, thrust my arms down in the same spot and, once again, they buckled, and I rolled forwards.

'Little Jacob's doing roly-polies,' I heard a voice snigger at

103

the back of the crowd and didn't need to look to know it was Blocker.

Saltham called, 'Again!'

Mortified, I went back to the start and took a deep breath, trying to visualize what my arms were going to do.

Tupai winked at me and Fizzer gave me a warm smile. 'You'll do it this time,' he said.

He was wrong. I managed to keep one arm straight, but the other buckled and threw me sideways, my feet smashing into Fizzer's chest. Well, where Fizzer's chest would have been if he hadn't sprung out of the way with that amazing athletic grace of his.

'Sorry,' I muttered for the second time.

Old Sea Salt strode forward and stood right in front of me, glaring. I was about to get blasted out of the water by a Navy Destroyer.

I stared back at him, trying desperately to get out of any further embarrassment. I focused my full power on his brain.

He can't do it, let him go. He can't do it, let him go.

Saltham shook his head, as if trying to clear it.

He can't do it, let him go. He can't do it, let him go.

It didn't work.

'Again!' he barked.

I grimaced and faced the ordeal.

And, as I looked and thought about it, I realized suddenly and with certainty, that I *could* do it. All I had to do was to keep my arms straight. Just focus on that one thing. Fizzer and Tupai would do the rest.

A feeling of confidence flooded over me. Of course I could do it. It was only nerves that had stopped me from succeeding before.

I flung myself forwards, dived on to the mat, my arms like rigid poles, sprang into the air, twisted perfectly over the outstretched arms of Fizzer and Tupai, and landed on my feet on the other side.

I almost expected applause, but there was none.

'Next,' said Saltham, and that was that. I just changed places with Tupai.

I did that exercise twice more, and had no further problems with it. It was funny, once I realized I could do it, it became easy.

In fact, I did it better than Blocker. He was OK, but he was so heavy that the other kids couldn't hold his weight, and he always ended up on his bum on the gym mat. It wasn't actually his fault, so Saltham didn't make him repeat the exercise, but I still felt a warm glow every time I did it right and he picked himself up off the mat.

At the end of PE most of the other kids got changed and wandered off to their next class, but I had a quick shower.

I didn't want to be sweaty and smelly after school when I met Erica in the library.

Her letter was zipped safely in an inside pocket of my school bag where I could touch it and bring it out to re-read in quiet moments, trying to read between the lines and work out what she was thinking from those few short words.

Meet me in the library after school on Friday. Erica.

The trouble was there wasn't a lot you could read into that.

I changed into my uniform and trotted off through the gym, rather pleased with myself for having conquered the difficult exercise.

Saltham was still there, working away at something on his clipboard.

I was feeling so pleased with myself that I actually smiled at him as I walked past, but he just glowered at me. I was almost out of the door before he spoke.

'Stay out of my head,' he said quietly, but then I was outside and I didn't turn back.

20

Frosty the Snow-Girl

The bell for last period sounded with a harsh trill; Maths had dragged on forever. I had taken off my watch for the last fifteen minutes of the period and placed it discreetly on my desk among my books where I could stare at it without it being too obvious.

The bell sounded like a jail-door opening. I was free. But almost immediately came another feeling. A jittery, flighty feeling in the pit of my stomach.

Why did Erica want to see me?

I threw my books into my school bag and was first out the door. I struggled not to run as I made for the library. No point. I'd have to wait for Erica anyway. Beautiful, icy Erica. At that point my mind started playing games with me.

She's already got a boyfriend, and he's seventeen. She's just going to laugh at you.

Then came another thought. *Why would you want to go out with her, anyway? Just because she's pretty? Maybe that's true, but who wants to go out with Frosty the Snow-girl? She may be pretty and smart, but where's her personality? She's just a big snob.*

And actually she isn't all that pretty when you think about it.

107

There are lots of girls who are better looking than her.

I tried to think of one but failed.

You don't really want to go out with her. No matter what she says, just tell her that you made a mistake; you didn't mean to say it.

Or even better . . .

Tell her you made a deal with Ben, and you only asked her out so that Ben would stand for student council.

That was it. Before she got a word in I was going to make it clear that I had no real interest in her. Then, when she gave me the bum's rush, or even if she let me down gently, it would be me who had turned her down.

I nodded my head to myself and scurried on towards the library. I had made up my mind.

The library was big, old and made of block and old brick, giving it the appearance of ramparts, almost like the castle I often felt it to be. I wandered around the shelves feigning interest in several subjects without even noticing what I was looking at. My legs were unsteady and my hands were quite shaky as I picked a few books off the shelves and put them back just as quickly.

I was glad Erica had suggested the library. It was the one place I felt most at home. Safe. Secure. I wondered why she had suggested it. I often saw her in there. Maybe she felt the same way, that it was a place of refuge.

Or, maybe, she just found it a quiet place to get away from all the other kids, and be aloof in her beautiful ivory tower.

She walked in while I was skimming through a book on ancient Peru and smiled nervously at me.

I forced my hands to be steady and smiled confidently back.

Confidence was important. I couldn't let her see how nervous I really was.

Now the trick was to let her down gently, before she could let me down.

She wandered over to the long couches at the New Zealand Fiction section of the library and I sheepishly followed her. She sat, and I sat on the couch opposite. Not next to her. There were a few kids in the library, doing homework or killing time till their parents picked them up, but where we were was deserted.

'Hi,' I said, trying to sound warm and friendly but in control of things.

'Hello,' Erica said and glanced down at her hands.

'First of all, thanks,' I said. 'Thanks for sending in the cavalry, the other day, at the GWF.'

'How did you know it was me?'

'I just guessed,' I said and took a deep breath. 'I thought I should tell you . . .' I tried to launch into my pre-prepared *I didn't mean it* speech but faltered, and she jumped right in.

'I guess you're wondering why I wrote that note,' she said.

My speech went right out of the window, and I just nodded mutely.

'I'm sorry about the other day,' she said, staring at her hands. 'You asked me if I wanted to go out with you . . .'

'Yes, but I was just . . .'

'I'm sorry I got upset.'

'My fault. But I was . . . I didn't really mean . . .'

'But nobody has ever asked me out before.'

I shut my mouth with a snap.

'And I wasn't really sure what to say.'

My mouth fell open again, and I stared at her. The most

beautiful creature on the planet and nobody had ever asked her out. (Yes, I know what I said before but I was just trying to convince myself, OK?)

'I heard you already had a boyfriend,' I said. 'I heard he was seventeen.'

She nodded and smiled, a little sadly I thought. 'I heard that one too.'

'But you're . . .' I hadn't intended it to go like this, but now it all came out in a rush, 'but you're beautiful. You're gorgeous. You're smart, you're . . . you're . . . I can't believe you haven't been asked out by lots of guys.'

She shook her head. 'Never.'

That was a real eye-opener. It dawned on me that we look at people and we judge them and decide what is going on inside their brains without ever getting to know them.

Erica wasn't icy. She wasn't aloof. She didn't consider herself better than the rest of us kids.

Erica was just shy!

No-one had ever asked her out before because, like me, they'd been frightened off by her looks and her intelligence.

I guess she was naturally shy, and that hadn't helped because it made her seem quite stand-offish.

And, I reasoned, the more other kids ignored her, the more isolated she became.

I said, 'My dad was a radio announcer, we moved around a lot.'

She looked up at me curiously.

I continued, 'I've been to five different schools in the last six years. Found it hard to make friends every time we moved.'

Her eyes widened. She drew in a sudden breath and said, 'Me too!'

I smiled at her; I had guessed as much.

She stared straight at me, for the first time, and the whole story came bubbling out. 'I was born here, but we moved back to Scotland when I was still a baby. Stayed there till I was eight. Then we returned to New Zealand. I had to leave all my friends behind, and all the new kids spoke funny, and they played different games and it took me ages to make any friends, and then, just when I did, we changed cities and . . . and . . .'

She looked like she was going to cry so I jumped right in. 'That's the story of my life. Except the bit about Scotland. And the part about kids speaking funny. And the games.'

She laughed, and the nearly-tears went away. She said, 'They told us that Kiwi kids were really friendly, but I never found that they were. And then all the other girls in the class started to get boyfriends, and nobody ever asked me, and I started to think that there must be something wrong with me.'

I changed couches and sat next to her. It felt like the right thing to do.

'There's nothing wrong with you,' I said. 'Not by a long way! I guess all the boys were just a bit afraid of you.'

'Except for you,' she said.

Just then didn't seem like the right time to tell her that I had been blackmailed into asking her out. So I didn't.

I said instead, 'So, um . . .'

'Yes?'

'Would you, um, go out with me?'

She turned to face me.

'Everyone says you're a trouble-maker. A loner.'

I held my breath.

'But I don't think it's true,' she said. 'I've seen the things you do.'

111

I looked seriously at her. 'You'll ruin my reputation if you tell anyone.'

She giggled. 'I won't say a word. And by the way, yes.'

It took me a moment or two to work out what the 'yes' meant.

And then I walked her home.

As I said, Erica didn't really live on my way home from school but she could have lived in Invercargill and I'd still have walked home with her.

Words are powerful things. They can start wars and stop them. They can change people's minds and change people's lives.

I didn't know it then, but those few words of mine, not particularly wise, not particularly wonderful, would change Erica's life. A few days later, she mustered up the courage to come out of her shell and made an effort to make friends with one of the girls in her class. And that was just the first step towards a whole new Erica.

21

Second Crime

You might have thought, with all this other stuff going on, that I had forgotten about my new career as a super-criminal. Well, I hadn't.

The great School Fair Robbery was still foremost on my mind, and my plans were slowly developing. But I needed information. Ben's first council meeting was at lunchtime on the Monday, and the fair was on the agenda.

Don't get this wrong. Ben knew nothing about what was going on. He was my unwitting accomplice in the crime, and I had to be careful how I wheedled the information out of him, so he wouldn't be too suspicious when all the money went missing.

My plans so far went like this. I knew the money would be kept somewhere on the school grounds until the end of the day, during which time it would be counted and sorted. At the end of the fair, it would be taken somewhere else for safekeeping, as the banks would be shut until the following Monday.

Somehow I was going to get myself into the counting room near the end of the day, and use my power to . . . well . . . I wasn't quite sure about that part yet, I still had to know the layout.

But my plan to get into the money room was simple. The only kids who would be allowed in would be those who were delivering the proceeds from their stalls.

So, I needed a small bucket of money. I would pretend it was from one of the stalls. I needed seed money. But now, at least, I knew where to get it.

Blocker had come to school on the Monday morning gloating about the hundred dollar note he had received for saving little Caitlin Howard's life. In his own mind, I think, he had reinvented history and had now even started to believe he had saved her, instead of just carrying her bag home. And, somehow, he had forgotten just who had chucked the rock.

If ever there was someone who deserved to lose a hundred dollars it was Blocker Blüchner.

Phil Domane was a different person that morning, though. He had also received a hundred dollars but there was no gloating from him. Quite the opposite, in fact. He seemed unusually withdrawn. Maybe it was guilt. Rumours about the truth of what had happened had already started circulating the school by the start of second period. Interval at Glenfield spreads information faster than the Internet!

Anyway, I noticed Ben getting a couple of claps on the back as he went into English, and you couldn't help but notice the kids staring at their shoes or turning away when Blocker pulled out his crisp new hundred dollar note and started bragging about what a hero he was.

I resolved to make that note mine before the end of the day.

Our English teacher was Miss Pepperman, naturally called

Peppermint by everyone she taught. She was young and funky, only about twenty-three or so, and she seemed to get on better with us kids than she did with some of the grey old ghosts who ran the rest of the school.

I got on especially well with her as we both found the English language endlessly fascinating.

We were studying a kind of Japanese poetry called haiku. Miss Peppermint told us all about an international haiku competition on the Internet. All year nines and tens were invited to enter. Miss Peppermint was going to judge the entries from our school, and the best one from each class was going to be entered in the competition.

The winner from our class, I decided, would be me.

When the period ended, I discreetly followed Blocker, trying to stay out of his sight by keeping at least two or three other kids in between us all the time.

He met up with Phil and another of their mates, Emilio, who was handsome and Spanish and as thick as two short planks. Emilio was carrying a rugby ball.

I noticed kids avoiding Blocker or turning their backs on him. News was spreading. I wondered how long it would take to reach Johnny Howard, Caitlin's big brother.

The three guys sat together to eat lunch, and I crept up close enough behind them to hear Emilio suggest a game of touch rugby.

'Yeah, let's go,' Blocker said when he had finished his sandwich.

What about the hundred dollar note? I suggested to his brain. *What about the hundred dollar note?*

He stopped, as if a thought had suddenly struck him. Which it had.

Don't want to lose it on the rugby field. Don't want to lose it on the rugby field.

I couldn't see his face, but his back suddenly straightened at that thought.

'I'll just go an' shove my bag in the classroom,' he said. 'Don't want to lose my hundred bucks, eh?'

Emilio laughed. A stupid braying laugh like a donkey. 'Who'd be stupid enough to steal money from you, Blocker? You'd smash their brains in.'

Phil was conspicuously silent.

'Yeah, you're right,' Blocker said.

Better be safe. Better be safe. Better be safe. I flashed the message as hard as I could at him.

'Better be safe, though, eh? Back in a minute.' With that, Blocker grabbed his bag and headed for our home room.

I skirted along the side of the building behind him, keeping out of his line of sight. Home room was ground level on B-Block and it was empty. Blocker flung the door open, crashing it against the wall with a splintering sound. Why? No good reason, I guess. He just seemed to enjoy mayhem and destruction. The automatic closer pulled the door shut behind him, and I snuck up to the glass panel set into the door to watch him.

He was on the far right side of the classroom, stuffing his bag into one of the wooden cubby-holes that lined the wall.

He pulled the money out from his pocket. A brand new but, by now, slightly wrinkled hundred dollar note, red and weighty with tremendous wealth. He looked around the room for somewhere to hide it.

I ducked down as he turned towards the door.

Dare I risk another peek? No. If he happened to catch me

looking in, and then the note went missing, he would do a real number on my carcass, Tupai or no Tupai.

Did my power work through walls? Did it work if I couldn't see the person I was trying to control? I had no idea.

I tried to visualize Blocker's ugly mug. It wasn't hard to do. The image that was the clearest was that of him a few inches from me, pounding his fist into my face as I lay on the canvas floor of the GWF ring.

Hide the money under the drunken Buddha. Hide the money under the drunken Buddha.

The Buddha was a decoration, a remnant of a senior school ball that had somehow found its way into our classroom. It was about a metre high and made of papier mâché over a wood and wire-netting base. The expression on its face was supposed to be one of serenity and peace, but whoever had made it hadn't done a great job, and it looked like it was drunk.

It was a great hiding place, nobody would ever think of looking there.

I rammed the thought home a couple more times. *Hide the money under the drunken Buddha, hide the money under the drunken Buddha.* When I heard movement, I ducked across the corridor into the toilets, closing the door silently behind me.

I heard Blocker's footsteps and then the outside door slam violently as he left. Did he always have to slam doors?

When I was certain he was well clear, I walked calmly into the room, trying hard not to act sneaky. It was my home room. I had a right to be there. I didn't have to creep around like some cartoon cat-burglar.

The Buddha sat on a long table that ran the length of the room near the cubby-holes. The rest of the table was filled with artwork and school projects.

I lifted the Buddha and, sure enough, there it was, the moustachioed face of Lord Rutherford. One hundred New Zealand dollars. The ill-gotten gains of Blocker Blüchner, now the loot of Super Freak.

'Moo-ha-ha-ha,' I chuckled an evil villain's laugh as I pocketed the note and replaced the Buddha.

Thirty seconds later I was eating my lunch with Ben in the courtyard and nobody had seen me do anything.

'Moo-ha-ha-ha.'

22

:-)

Next day at lunchtime I was sitting quietly with Ben, quizzing him about the council meeting the day before, when two things happened.

I had just found out that the money would be sorted and counted in the records room, before being locked in Principal Curtis's office for safety. *Perfect*, I thought, and then my mobile phone beeped with a text message.

'Probably Blocker being a dork again,' I said to Ben as I pulled it out of my bag.

I had just enough time to see that whoever the message was from, it wasn't Blocker, when Phil Domaine marched up right in front of us.

I braced myself for some kind of abuse, but it wasn't me he was after.

He said nothing, just thrust out an envelope towards Ben. 'What is it?' Ben asked, taking it hesitantly.

'It's yours,' Phil said and strode away without another word.

Ben looked at me and raised an eyebrow, then tore the end off the envelope. He shook out the contents. It was a brand new one hundred dollar note.

Not Blocker's, I had that, folded neatly into a back compartment of my wallet. It was Phil's.

'He shouldn't have done that,' Ben said. 'I'll give it back to him.'

'Yes, he should,' I said, quite amazed that he *had* actually done it. 'And, no, you bloody won't. It's yours. You keep it.'

Ben looked at it for a moment, then shrugged and put it in his pocket. 'I didn't expect to be paid for dragging that girl away from the wasps; it was just the right thing to do.'

At that moment, I was really proud to be Ben's friend, although I couldn't help wondering about my silly idea of him being a robot. He didn't seem to see things the same way as us humans.

I checked my text message. It was from Erica.

I hadn't seen her all day as we didn't have French, and my heart soared when I realized it was from her.

SO WHN R WE GOING OUT SMWHERE? She texted and added :-).

I hadn't thought about that. Now that we were officially going out, I supposed we needed some place to go out to. Perhaps the movies.

I started to text her back to suggest exactly that, when my phone beeped again. I eagerly opened the message expecting another gift from heaven.

But this was from the depths of hell.

U R DED MEAT.

I knew the number immediately.

The truth about Caitlin Howard must have eventually found its way to her big brother because Johnny went for Blocker in a big way after school.

It was down on bottom field, well away from the eyes of any teachers, and it was almost over by the time Ben and I got there.

Johnny was a rugby player and a bit of a tough nut, but Blocker was, well, Blocker. Johnny ended up in North Shore hospital with a dislocated shoulder.

Blocker had put two members of the same family in hospital within a week. I hope he felt proud.

Johnny never told on Blocker though. He never told his parents or any of the teachers just who had beaten him up. I suppose he couldn't.

After all, he had started it.

23

Dumbo Gumbo

There were three main groups of kids at Glenfield College: the popular kids, the regular kids and the rest of us. The leftovers.

Ben and I fell squarely into the third category and so, I suppose, did Erica, although she clearly belonged in the first category.

But things change rapidly with kids our age, and Ben and I somehow leapfrogged the middle group and jumped straight into the first. Not by choice I might add, but we were suddenly on the A list.

There were no secrets at Glenfield.

Ben sent Johnny an anonymous *Get Well* card in the hospital, and Johnny must have been surprised when he opened it and saw the money inside.

But I think Ben would have been even more surprised than Johnny if he had known that the envelope contained not one, but two hundred dollar bills.

It was all very secretive, but, somehow, whispers echoed along corridors and skimmed across the concrete of the courtyards. Ben was widely applauded, partly for his heroism in rescuing the girl, but mostly for his humility in wanting neither reward nor recognition for his deed.

All I had done was to take the school bully down a notch or two, but it was enough to award me school legend status. The school grapevine had heard about Blocker's missing money and, perhaps because of the GWF, guessed I had something to do with it.

Tom Prebble came up to me in the hall foyer and shook my hand. 'Good on ya,' he said, with a knowing wink.

I started to ask what he was talking about, but he just tapped his nose with his finger and walked on.

I hoped Blocker wouldn't come to the same conclusion. Still, that Robin Hood feeling was back and it was pretty cool to be popular. Strange, but very very cool.

It caused some problems, though, and I actually found myself regretting all the attention. Here was I, trying to plan the crime of the century and, suddenly, I was an object of attention wherever I went.

On Friday I asked Erica out to the movies. Not via text (I had decided against that idea) but in person.

She accepted immediately and seemed very excited at the idea of going to the movies. With me. Jacob John Smith.

The fact that the most beautiful girl in school was *excited* at the idea of going on a date with me did wonders for my ego, I can tell you.

After that, we started texting each other regularly. Never during class though, which would risk having your phone confiscated. And I never kept any of the text messages. I deleted them as soon as I received them, fearing they would fall into the wrong hands.

I did keep all of Blocker's texts, thinking that they might one day be used in evidence against him.

That turned out to be a big mistake, but how was I to know?

Blocker had his suspicions about the hundred dollar note, I was sure of that, and my fears were confirmed when he suddenly upped the intimidation level.

I was leaving school on my own, as Ben was at a student council meeting, when I noticed Blocker and Phil standing outside the gates. Waiting. For me.

I ignored them and walked straight past. Two strides later, I realized they were following me. Not just following, shadowing, half a pace behind. I could almost feel Blocker's cheesy breath on the back of my neck.

I tired of this after a few metres, stepped to the side and stopped to let them past.

They stopped in synch with me, and waited, right behind me. I didn't turn around. I didn't want to give them the satisfaction. I just waited a while, then started off again.

Phil and Blocker followed, right at my heels.

It sounds stupid the way I've described it, like a kids' game. But it wasn't. It was terrifying. I felt that any moment there would be a smashing blow to the back of my head or a paralyzing kick to my kidneys.

I tried to use my power, but it had no effect. Either they were too determined or I was too unnerved to concentrate properly.

They said nothing until we reached my front gate. Dad was hammering away on some old piece of furniture in the garage and Gumbo came rushing out, barking like a mad thing.

He jumped up on me, slobbering like crazy, and knocked me back a step. I collided with Blocker, who shoved me off with a grunt.

'What a nice doggie,' he said, with a mile-wide sneer in his voice.

I couldn't help but glance around, and something about the way Blocker was looking at Gumbo sent a chill right through me.

Gumbo must have picked it up, too, because he took one look at Blocker and growled, a low rumbly sound from deep in his throat. His lips drew back, baring his teeth in a vicious snarl. I'd never seen him do that in his entire life.

Gumbo, the sometimes scary, farty, sporty, floppy, sloppy dog.

'Let's get out of here,' Phil said urgently.

Blocker acted as if he wasn't scared.

'Come on, Gumbo,' I said quickly and grabbed him by the collar.

Blocker began to back away. 'Gumbo and Dumbo,' he laughed, as he and Phil retreated cautiously. 'Dumbo and Gumbo.'

That was it. That was all it took. Gumbo broke free from my grip and charged at Blocker.

Blocker and Phil spun around and ran for their lives.

They sprinted down the road with their schoolbags flying out behind them. Gumbo lunged along after them, barking and growling, and I ran along behind yelling, 'Gumbo, come back!' It must have looked quite a sight.

Gumbo couldn't catch them; he was old, and his legs tired quickly. Pretty soon I had him, and we walked back home, while Blocker jeered at us and made rude signs from the safety of the far side of the main road.

Ben rang me about half an hour later, excited out of his brain. 'You know that photo we took of the lightning strike?'

'The photo *you* took . . .'

'Well . . . yeah. It was entered in the annual *Sunday Star Times* photo competition and it won the junior section!'

'Fantastic!'

'It's going to be printed in the paper!'

'Good on ya.'

'It'll be huge. Half the back page of the first section.'

'Well done, mate!' I was genuinely pleased for him.

But I still had a few problems of my own to contend with.

24

Will Bender

The door opened slowly on to a room filled with unimaginable treasures.

'Come,' had been the single word response to my hesitant knock.

Mr Saltham's office was at the back of the old hall, beneath what had once been the stage. School mythology said that nobody had ever seen Old Sea Salt's office and lived, so I hoped I would be the first. To survive I mean.

On every available space there were marvels. An antique naval globe shared space with an old-fashioned sextant. A brass compass sat next to a plaque with a photo of a large navy ship of some kind. One shelf held a painstakingly detailed model of a sailing ship, the *Victory*, according to the name on its side. Hanging on a chain from the ceiling was one of those old-fashioned metal diver's helmets with the big round faceplates.

I had to skirt around a huge brass telescope on a wooden tripod to approach Mr Saltham's desk. As I did, I noticed a photo of a very young Mr Saltham receiving a medal from the Queen of England.

I didn't know much about the royal navy, and even less

about their medals, but I didn't have to be a genius to work out that, if the medal was being presented by the Queen, then it was a serious piece of tin.

I suddenly realized there was a lot more to Old Sea Salt than just the grumpy old guy who ran the Glenfield College gym.

His desk was covered with more of the same: miniature ensigns; a tiny brass cannon paperweight; and a clock shaped like the steering wheel of an old sailing ship.

Mr Saltham hadn't left the navy at all. He had brought it with him.

'Jacob,' he said, and I was surprised he used my first name. Saltham called everyone by their surname, and I, if he noticed me at all, was usually 'Smith.'

'Excuse me,' I said nervously. 'I was hoping for a word.'

He stared at me and did not invite me to sit, although there was a spare seat in front of the desk.

I began, 'I, er . . .'

'I know what it's about, Jacob,' he said. 'And I was wondering when you'd show up.'

This was not going as I had expected it to. He sounded almost friendly.

'The other day you said something . . . I may have heard you wrong . . . but something that sounded a little like: "Stay out of my head." I wondered what you meant.'

'You know damn well what I meant.'

'I um . . .'

'Don't you try any more of your psychic tricks on me. You only got me that first time because I wasn't expecting it. I hadn't seen it for a few years.'

I sat down in shocked silence.

'You mean there are others . . .?'

Saltham began to laugh. 'So, you thought you were the only one! That's rich. You all like to think you are so special.'

'How many others are there?' I asked incredulously.

'How the hell should I know,' was Saltham's testy response. 'I don't keep a register of these things. I've seen perhaps four or five kids come through the school with your sort of ability. "Will Benders" I call you, because of the way you try to make other people do what you want. Most of them were just like you, although there was one young lady who had an incredible ability.'

He paused for a moment, remembering, then shot back to me. 'Let me guess. You can suggest things; you can put thoughts into people's minds and make them think they've thought of it themselves. But you can't convince someone to do something they wouldn't do otherwise or if they're determined not to do it. You couldn't make someone jump off a cliff, for example. Sound pretty much right?'

I nodded. As far as I knew he had it right on the button.

'If you've seen four or five of us . . .' It felt weird saying *us*. 'Then there must be others, in other schools, in other countries . . .'

'Thousands, I'd say.'

'But that's impossible. We'd have heard about it. It would have been on the news or in *Time* or CNN or something.'

Old Sea Salt smiled at me. 'And how many people have you told?'

I said nothing. He was right, of course.

He continued. 'Besides, I reckon half of them don't even know they have the power. Not unless they've consciously tried to use it.'

My head was spinning with all this information.

'You can always pick them,' he was saying. I tried to focus on his words. 'People in the news, in positions of power, people who seem to have a strange effect on the people around them. Think about it. You'll come up with a whole list.'

I tried, but my mind was a blank. 'But how come you can tell?' I asked, although the answer was already beginning to dawn on me. 'How come you spotted me so quickly?'

'Takes one to know one,' Saltham said, and roared again with laughter.

Then it all made sense.

The somersault exercise. I had failed and failed again. I had been convinced I would fail, and then, suddenly, I had been sure I would succeed. That I could do it.

'It was you,' I said slowly. 'You made me feel confident.'

Saltham stood up and said, 'I've got to get to the staffroom.'

He held the door open for me. I ducked beneath his arm and started to climb the spiral wooden staircase up to the wings of the old stage.

Saltham called up.

'You're going to have to make a choice now, Jacob. What to do with it. Your power. Or if you're going to do anything at all.'

His voice echoed up out of the gloom. 'Some people have the ability their whole lives and know it, but never use it. They don't think it's right to try to control and manipulate people.'

He repeated, 'You're going to have to make a choice.'

I shook my head, which hurt from all this sudden and terrifying new information.

And the Spring Fever School Fair was rapidly approaching.

25

Turning the Tables

The next week, Blocker followed me home every night. Three times with Phil and once without. They stopped now at the end of my road, to avoid Gumbo, but it was still nerve-wracking, and I was getting sick of it. They didn't seem to care if I was with Ben or not.

Ben wanted to turn around and face them, but I didn't want to start a fight.

On the Friday, I had been intending to walk home with Erica, but I sent her a text, making an excuse. I didn't want her to have to endure Blocker and Phil's attention. By now, I was so worked up about it I decided to change the rules of the game. I was mad at having to walk home feeling frightened, and I was mad at missing out on walking home with Erica.

So I turned the tables on them.

I asked Ben to walk home by himself and explained why. He nodded and trotted mechanically off. I hid behind some trees by the side of A-Block and watched Blocker and Phil watching Ben walk away.

They were pretty persistent. They waited until nearly four o'clock for me before giving up and heading off.

I snuck out from behind the trees and followed them.

Look straight ahead, I thought at them. *Don't look back.*

Old Saltham might not feel comfortable about trying to control those around him, but I had no such qualms. Especially when it came to Blocker Blüchner.

Blocker and Phil kept their eyes straight ahead. They never even glanced at each other while they talked about sports and the GWF.

I grew more and more daring as we walked and kept up a constant flow of the *look straight ahead* messages. I walked closer and closer behind them, almost as close as they had been doing to me.

I dropped back a bit though when they turned down the short lane into Acorn Park. No sense in being silly about it.

They passed the old stump, now fumigated by the council and dead as a doorknob, and followed the concrete path through the trees.

At that point Blocker said, 'How about a game of Bench Seat Hockey?'

Phil just shook his head, but that didn't discourage Blocker. They approached a long wooden bench seat in the park and Blocker, with some disgusting noises in the back of his nose and throat, summonsed up an almighty hock, which he spat on to the seat with relish, right where anyone would sit.

I screwed my face up.

'Hockey one!' Blocker cried, triumphantly.

The next bench seat was 'Hockey two,' and the next 'Hockey three,' and then they were out of the park, but that didn't stop Blocker. They passed a bus stop, and that seat got the *hockey* treatment.

'I am the hock-meister,' Blocker yelled.

I was disgusted, and I don't think Phil was all that impressed either. He wasn't saying anything, but there was something about the shape of his shoulders which gave me an idea.

Blocker was going on about what a dumb-ass Tupai White was, and how he could thrash him if he didn't always have his friends around him. It was utter crap, but I think Blocker almost believed it.

They got to the next bus stop, and Blocker hocked it good, then threw his head back and crowed, 'Hock-a-doodle do.'

I aimed my full power at the back of Phil's head.

What a jerk. What a jerk. What a jerk.

I guess I was aiming to sow a bit of disharmony in the ranks of my enemy, but I was unprepared for the reaction.

Phil said with a great depth of feeling, 'You're a jerk sometimes, Blocker.'

Blocker froze. I ducked into someone's driveway and hid behind a pohutukawa tree.

'What?' Blocker said incredulously.

'You're a real jerk,' Phil said, and I noticed he had left out the 'sometimes'.

'What the hell is wrong with you, all of a sudden?'

Phil looked suddenly nervous, but he didn't back down. 'All this seat bench stuff, it's stupid. And following the frea . . . Jacob . . . home every day. What's the point?'

'Are you whoossing out on me?' Blocker loomed over Phil, who was tall and strong but not as big as Blocker.

'Just grow up a bit.'

'You dirt-bag!' Blocker grabbed Phil by the shirt.

'Get off me, you loser!' Phil shouted, and that was when Blocker hit him.

Phil hit him back, hard, and Blocker doubled up for a

133

second but, before Phil could do anything else, Blocker charged at him, bowling him over into a flower garden and raining punches on to him.

I didn't know what to do. I hadn't expected this at all.

Phil was hitting back but he was out of his weight division and he was pinned underneath. I could see he was in a lot of trouble, which had been my intention, but not quite like this.

At that point the front door of the house next door opened and a face I recognized came running out. It was Jenny Kreisler from our class.

'Get off him,' she shrieked. 'Leave him alone!'

That didn't help at all. It was a right old scrap, and Phil was clearly getting the worst of it.

I almost came running out to help, although I was sure that would only make matters worse, when Jenny marched right up to them, grabbed Blocker by the hair and wrenched him off.

He nearly took a swing at her in his rage but stopped himself just in time.

'Get out of here!' Jenny shrieked at him. Other doors were starting to open now, lace curtains were being drawn back. Blocker stumbled off, mumbling to himself.

Phil hadn't moved.

I was quite a few metres away down the street and still out of sight, so I just stayed put as Jenny helped Phil to his feet and took him inside her house. His face was a bloody mess.

When her door was closed, I casually walked by as if I had seen nothing.

I wasn't at all sure whether to feel guilty or not.

26

My First Date

That Saturday night I took Erica to the movies. I dressed in my best jeans and a trendy, but second-hand, jacket, which had taken what little savings I had. What did it matter? I reasoned. I would soon have as much money as I could spend.

I went to the garage to get my bike and noticed that one of Dad's tools was missing. A chisel, judging by the empty black outline left on the pegboard. That was a little strange, as he always put everything back. I knew he wasn't using it, because he was out at his *Shortland Street* audition.

The *Shortland Street* audition! I had forgotten all about it in my excitement. There seemed to be so many good things happening at the moment, and if Dad won the audition then that would just cap it all off!

I cycled to Erica's place, and we caught the bus into the city. I didn't really like the idea of catching the bus, it wasn't very romantic, but we didn't have much choice.

Dad always said that real people travelled by bus. Th' you never met anyone interesting sitting alone in a car. (he said, you plugged directly into the pumpi' humanity.

But I think he just said that because we couldn't afford a car.

I'd never been on a date with a girl and I wasn't sure what to do. I mean, did it involve kissing and stuff? In the end, we went to the big Sky City Multiplex and sat in comfortable leather chairs. About half way through the movie Erica's hand slipped quietly into mine, and we just stayed like that while Jennifer Love Hewitt got really upset about something I couldn't understand and Will Smith took his shirt off a lot.

Afterwards, Erica gave me a quick peck on the cheek, like the darting glance of a bird, before the bus came, and that, really, was that.

My first date.

27

Dry Run

In preparation for the school fair, tonnes of items had poured in for the huge white elephant stall. The flotsam and jetsam of households throughout the school's catchment area. It was like a gigantic garage sale.

I passed piles of the stuff heaped up on the netball court on Monday morning, and on Monday afternoon kids were asked to volunteer to help sort and price it.

Ben automatically volunteered. Part of his duty as a student councillor, I suppose. I stuck my hand up, too, although I had reasons of my own.

Big things like lawnmowers and bicycles, bed frames and old washing machines were being moved around.

As far as I could tell, they were just taking stuff from one pile and putting it in another, without improving things at all. But I suppose they had a plan.

Blocker and Phil were both helping. I suspect all the rugby teams had been drafted in to help with the heavier items. I noticed that Phil had a black eye and a sliver of sticking plaster across his lip. He didn't talk to Blocker at all, and the silence was returned tenfold.

I had to get closer to Blocker than I would have liked when one of the parent helpers asked the two of us to pick up each end of a rusty barbecue. I kept my face blank, but Blocker was not so circumspect. He scowled at me, and his eyes were black with malice.

Something was brewing inside him, and I was afraid of what would happen when it finally boiled over. Emilio had changed schools and Blocker didn't really have any other friends, apart from Phil. I knew what that was like and I could almost feel sorry for him.

Blocker and I placed the barbecue where we were told and, with a small sigh of relief, I went to look for something else to do.

Ben was trying to lift an old toilet pan but it was a bit too heavy for him, so I went to give him a hand. I hoped it was clean!

We shoved a few things here and there under the directions of the parent-helpers, and, the whole time, my mind was on my special power. On what Saltham had said.

How many people have you told?

We stopped for a drink of water after about an hour, and that was when I finally told my best friend in the world, my biggest secret in the world.

'Have you ever tried to control someone's mind?' I asked him.

'What do you mean?' Ben asked, with a slightly worried expression.

'Like, tried to make someone think certain thoughts, just by focusing your own thoughts on their brain.'

'No.'

'Do you think you would be able to?'

'No.'

'I can.'

There was silence while he thought about it for a while.

I said, 'Do you remember when Frau Blüchner wrote "knickers" on the blackboard? I made her do that.'

'No way!' Ben exclaimed.

'Yep. I'll prove it if you want.'

'OK, make me think of something.'

'OK then.'

He looked at me and I focused myself on his brain and thought.

Chocolate Ice-cream, Chocolate Ice-cream, Chocolate Ice-cream.

'Are you doing it?' he asked.

'Yes, what are you thinking about at the moment?' I asked confidently.

He shook his head. 'About how stupid you look when you frown like that.'

I was a bit surprised. 'Really?'

'Yeah.'

I thought for a moment. 'OK, I'll try again.'

Scratch your nose, scratch your nose, scratch your nose.

Ben blinked a couple of times but that was it. 'You're having me on about this aren't you?'

'No!' I insisted. 'Look, let me try it on someone else.' I looked around and saw Jordan Hoffman-Herbert treading his way carefully amongst an old china tea-set spread out on a tartan picnic rug.

'See Jordan over there. I'll make him pick up the cup with the broken handle, then put it back down again.'

Ben watched. I concentrated.

Pick up the broken cup.

After a second Jordan bent down and picked up the cup with the broken handle.

It's no good, put it back down.

He placed it back on the rug.

'And again,' I said.

Pick it up again, put it down again.

Jordan picked the cup up, as if noticing it for the first time, then replaced it.

'Wow,' Ben said.

Pick it up, put it down.

I tried to make him do it a third time, but he turned away.

'Believe me now?' I asked.

Ben stared at me, not sure what to think. One thought was troubling me though. My power hadn't worked on Ben at all. Maybe he had been concentrating too hard. It seemed to work best when people weren't concentrating. As if, somehow, I could slip thoughts into absent minds.

But then again, I suppose you wouldn't expect it to work on a robot, would you?

Smaller or more valuable items, like crockery and cutlery, clocks and old jewellery were taken to the staff-room to sort out. I put a few such things into a cardboard carton and headed in that direction.

I went via the entrance from the foyer. It took longer, but I did it deliberately.

I walked through the doors into the admin block. On Fair Day there would be a security guard of some sort here. But that was part of my plan, and I knew how I would deal with it.

I passed Curtis's office where the money would be stored for safe-keeping and barely glanced at the records room, where

140

the counting would be done. Through the window I saw Mr Saltham walk into the staffroom, and I cringed inside and half-ducked, but he didn't see me.

My plan was beautiful in its simplicity. It was elegant, ingenious, and almost fool-proof.

Unfortunately, I wasn't totally convinced now that I actually wanted to go through with it. I was feeling troubled as I took my box into the staff room and placed it on a table with a bunch of other boxes filled with similar bric-a-brac.

Through the window I saw Erica in the distance, walking with Stacey Anderson and Chelsie Burnett. She was relaxed and happy, and I felt an incredible warmth just watching her. She was talking with her hands. It was a habit of hers, I had discovered, once she felt comfortable with you. While she was nervous and shy her hands stayed by her side but, once she relaxed, then those hands started flying around.

I liked it. It made her seem lively and animated. And it was good to see her getting on so well with Stacey and Chelsie. I had whispered in a few ears about how shy Erica was and that she was really nice once you got to know her.

A few weeks ago, nobody would have listened to Jacob the Freak. But Jacob the Hero was a different story.

Watching Erica walk by with her new friends gave me a good feeling inside. A big, warm, fuzzy emotion that I didn't know the name for.

28

Detention Times Two

Erica sat on the opposite side of the detention room and smiled at me across the top of the book she was reading.

There was no essay today. Mrs Pepperman was in charge of detention, and, like me, she didn't believe in writing as a form of punishment. Instead, she said we could read for the half hour.

It was pretty strange, sitting in detention with Erica McDonald. I mean, it was strange for her to be there. The detention room was almost my second home, but this was Erica's first detention.

I hadn't really done anything wrong. I had just mucked up my time-table and turned up for one class when I was supposed to be at another class, which was on the other side of the school. So, I had walked in ten minutes late and got slapped with a detention.

I don't think the crime deserved the punishment, and I did have a good reason, but, by now, some teachers seemed to be so used to giving me detention that it just happened automatically. Maybe I was on a blacklist somewhere.

Erica was in detention because of the missing ferret affair.

What had happened was this.

Jenny Kreisler had had a rabbit named George, but it had died. Sandra Greathouse was getting a guinea pig but didn't have a cage to keep it in, so Jenny had offered to lend her George's travel cage.

Jenny brought the cage to school and left it beside her desk in history while she went to get something from her locker.

Doddery old Mr Toppler walked in and tripped over the cage, knocking it half way across the room.

'What's this doing here?' he demanded angrily.

Erica just happened to be standing there, and I guess she had been hanging around me too long and something must have rubbed off, because she said, on the spur of the moment, 'That's my ferret Wilbur.'

'Ferret?' Mr Toppler said, rubbing his ankle. 'What ferret?'

Erica rushed around the front of her desk and clapped her hands to her face. She squealed, 'Oh, no! Wilbur's escaped.'

Mr Toppler wasted no time. 'Quickly children,' he shouted, 'find that ferret before it gets out of the classroom.'

The kids thought this sounded like much more fun than another boring history lesson, and quickly began searching under desks, inside school bags and cupboards, as if they thought there really was a ferret, although they were, of course, all in on the joke.

Jenny came back from her locker to find her classmates tearing the room apart and trying not to giggle. She joined in the hunt immediately.

'What are we looking for?' she asked.

'The ferret's got loose,' Erica told her, with a wink.

'Erica,' Mr Toppler cried, 'go to the office and get them to announce it over the intercom.'

So Erica did exactly that, and pretty soon the entire school was being turned upside down. They even had groups of students scouring the perimeter and the playing fields. Nearly a whole period was wasted before they figured it out.

Mr Toppler was outraged and Erica ended up in front of the principal. She probably would have received a stronger punishment than she did, but Mr Curtis could hardly keep a straight face, so she got off with a detention.

Which is why we were sitting there on the Wednesday afternoon making eyes at each other over our reading books.

She scribbled a note quickly on a scrap of paper and held it against the back of her book, so that only I could see it. *I ♥ U*, it said.

I smiled broadly at her by way of a response. She held up another note. *It's my birthday tomorrow, what are you getting me?*

I winked at her as if I knew that already and had the whole thing planned, although, of course, I had no idea.

It took me three jewellery shops in a mad scrambling dash after school to find what I was looking for, but I found it. It pretty much cleaned out the rest of my life-savings, but the gift was perfect.

I gave it to her the next day before school, all wrapped in pretty blue paper and tied with a bow (gift-wrapped by the jeweller's assistant). Erica opened it and burst out laughing. It was a delicate silver chain with a little silver pendant, in the shape of a ferret. I laughed with her.

Turned out the joke was on me, though. It wasn't really her birthday at all.

She's a trouble-maker, that Erica.

29

Catastrophe

The Friday of that week, the day before the school fair, started off badly, got steadily worse, and by lunchtime was an unmitigated catastrophe.

It was sunny and warm, a lovely spring morning. Gumbo was sleeping on the end of my bed. I was at a school where I felt, for the first time since primary, that I fitted in, and had friends.

Even Blocker had stopped hassling me.

It seemed that all was right with the world.

The phone rang at 7:30 and Dad answered it. After a short greeting, he went silent. I knew something was wrong. He hung up the phone brusquely and stomped up the hall to the kitchen. A few moments later he was having a stand-up row with Mum.

I made my bed extra-nice and tidied my room. It was the sort of morning that I'd get it in the neck if I put a single foot out of place.

April just locked her door and stayed there. She'd skip breakfast to avoid the drama. Chicken.

I could already hear what the problem was. Dad had missed

out on the *Shortland Street* role. All that mangled English for nothing.

It wouldn't have been so bad if he hadn't been so confident that he would get it; that his time as an actor had come. And we had all fallen under the spell of his confidence and started dreaming of riches and luxuries.

I went quietly to the kitchen for breakfast but Dad yelled at me for slamming the fridge and then Mum yelled at him for yelling at me, saying it wasn't my fault he'd missed out on the audition.

Maybe April had had the right idea.

Second period was English with Miss Pepperman. As always I felt more cheerful when I walked into her classroom. Her personality brightened the whole classroom, and I thought that if we had more teachers like her, there'd be fewer problems in schools.

Or did all teachers start off like her when they were young? Maybe even old Frau Blüchner had once been a young excited inspirational teacher to her classes.

Maybe, but it was hard to believe.

It was the results day for the class haiku competition. I had put a little time aside from all my criminal activities and written the best haiku I could. I thought it was pretty good.

Flowing water falls
Leading to the salty sea
I don't want to fall

It didn't win though. In the end Miss Pepperman couldn't choose between two poems and was going to send them both off for the international competition. Neither of them was mine.

One was a mournful piece by Jenny Kreisler, pining for a lost love. The other, to my jaw-dropping amazement, was by Blocker Blüchner.

Fast rushing water
Swooping down, hitting sharp rocks
Leaving bleeding scars

Losing to Blocker surprised me and stung me in ways I didn't expect. I think Blocker was a bit surprised too and scowled at anyone who even looked as though they might be going to congratulate him.

Stephen Wilson from 3G came in with a note for Miss Pepperman just before lunchtime, and she read it carefully twice, frowning each time, before thanking Stephen and sending him on his way.

She looked around the class. 'Take out your reading books; we'll have SSR for the rest of the period.' That was Sustained Silent Reading. 'Except you, Jacob.'

I looked up in fright. *Except me! Why?*

'Jacob, pack up your schoolbag and come with me.'

Now I was really worried. Had somebody died?

'What's going on?' I asked, as she walked with me towards the admin block.

'I don't know,' she tried to give me a reassuring smile.

The door to Principal Curtis's office was shut. When she knocked, the door was pulled open abruptly by someone inside. Miss Pepperman gave me another of those not-so-reassuring smiles and left me to it. I wished she could stay.

Sitting on the old leather sofa just inside the door were my parents. *This was not a good sign.*

I inched inside, and it got worse. Mr Curtis was staring sternly at me. Mr Saltham stood in the center of the room.

Seated in the far corner of the office was Frau Blüchner, and the look on her face was venomous.

Mum smiled at me, a little tentatively, but Dad just sat there. I guess he was having a bad day all round.

Mr Curtis didn't invite me to sit, so I just stood in front of the desk, holding my schoolbag. Mr Saltham closed the door.

There was a silence for a little while, but it was silence heavy with menace, like those swollen black clouds you get just before it rains.

'Jacob,' Curtis said severely, 'a very serious charge has been made against you by another student.'

All I could think about was my planned crime. But I hadn't done anything yet!

'This student says you threatened to kill him. That you attacked him with a knife.'

'A chisel!' corrected Mrs Blüchner.

'It's not true!' I burst out, although I had a horrible feeling who was behind this and where it was going.

'Are you calling him a liar?' Mrs Blüchner fumed, and if it wasn't obvious before who the complainant was, it was clear as day now.

Dad still said nothing, but Mum's face was granite and her eyes were steel.

'Are you calling my son a liar?'

Curtis interrupted before the two women could go head to head.

'Empty your bag out please, Jacob.'

'Is this necessary?' Mum wanted to know.

Curtis nodded mutely.

With a cold feeling of dread I emptied my schoolbag. One by one, I laid each article on the desk in front of me. Dad still hadn't said anything, which was the most frightening thing of all.

I emptied my bag and Curtis peered through the minutiae of my school life. There was nothing incriminating. *Phew!!!* He even opened my pencil case and looked inside.

'There you go,' Mum said, as if that was the end of that. 'As I said before . . .'

Saltham reached out and took the bag from me, as Mum rattled on about how I would never do such a thing.

He flattened it on the desk and pressed down on it, then, with a strange look on his face, he opened it and felt around inside until he found the inside compartment.

I hadn't opened that. I never used it.

Saltham unzipped it and pulled out a long yellow handled chisel with JS, my dad's initials, burnt into the handle. The missing chisel from our garage.

'Crikey!' said Mum.

Saltham laid it on Curtis's desk where it stared up at all of us.

'Is this yours?' he asked my father. Dad nodded and looked at me strangely.

'That doesn't mean anything,' Mum said.

Mr Curtis said, 'Anything you want to tell me?'

'It's not mine,' I said.

Curtis looked at Dad.

I said quickly, 'I mean I didn't put it there. It went missing from our garage. I didn't put it in my bag and I certainly didn't attack anyone with it.'

Mrs Blüchner was doing her volcano thing and just about to erupt, but Curtis held up a hand for her to be silent.

'You're saying you didn't threaten anyone with this.'

I had just said that, hadn't I!

'Absolutely not!'

Curtis looked up at Saltham, who said, 'He was pretty clear about what had happened. Better get him in here and get him to tell you directly.'

Curtis pressed a button on the intercom and said, 'Send for the other boy.'

Then he looked at my parents and said, 'We'll sort this out right now.'

I tried to say, 'Blocker, I mean Markus, has been following me home after school. He must have seen the tools . . .'

But Curtis cut me off. 'You'll get your turn to talk.'

A moment later, Blocker entered and we both stood in front of the desk. Blocker towering over me.

'Tell us what happened, Markus,' Mr Curtis said gently. 'Tell us what you told Mr Saltham.'

It should have been obvious to anyone that Blocker had prepared this.

He said calmly, 'Yesterday afternoon after school I was walking home through Acorn Park and Jacob jumped out from behind a tree. He said he was going to kill me if I didn't leave him alone and took a swing at me with the chisel.'

My jaw dropped open. It was total bull-crap. I looked around. They were buying it! All of them. Even Mum and Dad.

I stared out of the window, isolated in my frustration and despair.

Curtis said, 'What did he mean, "If you didn't leave him alone"?'

Blocker looked suitably sorrowful. 'Well, I guess I'd been razzing him a bit.'

'Bullying?' asked Mr Curtis sharply.

Blocker shrugged. 'I guess. I don't mean to. It's my size. Some of the smaller kids just seem scared of me.' He stared at the floor as if in pain. 'It's hard to make friends sometimes.'

I could not believe what I was hearing. 'This is so . . .'

'You'll get your turn!' Mrs Blüchner's voice, wrung out through clenched teeth, cut me off like a guillotine.

Blocker continued. 'I did send him a few nasty text messages. But that was only because I'd heard he'd stolen my money.'

'The money he was given for rescuing that girl!' Mrs Blüchner thundered.

'All right, Jacob,' Curtis said. 'Tell us why you did it.'

'I didn't do it.' I said simply.

'You have no proof of any of this.' Dad finally found his voice and started to talk in a smooth, lawyerly tone.

Curtis picked up my mobile phone from amongst the jumble of my belongings on his desk. He pressed a few buttons and then read out one of Blocker's text messages, 'You are dead meat.'

'I didn't mean it,' Blocker said quickly. 'It's just stuff that kids say.'

Curtis nodded, agreeing with him. I was raging inside, but unable to do or say anything.

Somehow, those text messages from Blocker seemed to prove his side of the story. That I'd attacked him with a chisel because he had been bullying me.

'Do you want to give me any good reasons why you did this?' Curtis asked. It seemed there was no doubt about whether I had in fact done it.

'I didn't do it!' I shouted.

'He's a strange kid,' Blocker butted in. 'Calls himself the Freak.'

Mum and Dad looked at each other in surprise at that revelation.

Actually it was Super Freak, but I didn't think it would help to tell them that.

Curtis raised an eyebrow at me.

'Only because . . .' I tailed off, there was no way of explaining it. The whole GWF thing and the special power.

I looked desperately at Dad. Where was my defence council when I needed him? Mum was strong, but by herself she was seriously mismatched against the panzer tank in the corner.

Still, Mum did her best, and for the next ten minutes butted heads with Frau Blüchner. She didn't really stand a chance, though.

Finally Curtis seemed to make up his mind. He looked firstly at Blocker. 'Bullying is a serious offence in this school,' he intoned slowly. 'If I hear any more about you bullying other kids, by phone, or any other way, I will be forced to take further action. Do you understand me?'

'Yes, sir,' Blocker nodded meekly. Inside he must have been laughing fit to bust.

'Jacob,' Curtis paused thoughtfully, 'I'm sorry, but I cannot condone this offence. If you felt threatened by another student you should have talked to a teacher or a school counsellor. Violence is not the answer.'

My face was red. Red with fury at the injustice of it all. Red with frustration at how other people were controlling my life.

Curtis finished, 'I have no choice but to suspend you from school for two weeks.'

He looked calmly at my parents. 'You might want to think about finding Jacob another school. He may not be coming back.'

30

Spring Fever

Funnily enough, I think Mum and Dad believed me. At least they weren't as angry with me as I would have expected.

'Did you do it, mate?' Mum asked once, just once.

'No.' I shook my head sadly and that was good enough for her.

I was still trying to comprehend the scale of the catastrophe. I was probably going to be kicked out of school, just when I had started to fit in. I'd be in a different school to Ben. And Erica.

This was a disaster beyond imagination.

On Saturday morning, however, I woke up full of determination. I wasn't going to let other people run my life. I was going to the school fair, suspension or no suspension, and I was going to rob them blind. Serve them bloody well right and all. The crime of the century was now an act of revenge.

I listened to the weather forecast. It was for thunder-storms. There was no sign of them yet, though, the morning was hazy and warm. I hoped the storms stayed away. I wanted the school fair to be a good one. A highly *profitable* one.

Moo-ha-ha-ha.

I showered and dressed then wandered into the kitchen for breakfast. I was the only one up, which suited me fine.

The only one apart from Gumbo, who was lying down staring at the TV.

'The Warriors aren't playing until next week,' I told him.

He looked at me, farted, and went back to watching the blank screen.

'Crazy dog,' I muttered, making myself some toast.

Gumbo, the lazy, crazy, sometimes scary, farty, sporty, floppy, sloppy dog. And I loved him.

'I'll buy you a present when I'm rich,' I promised, but he ignored me and continued watching the blank screen.

The fair didn't start till ten, but I cycled off as soon as I had finished breakfast. I wanted to be out of the house before Mum and Dad got up and started quizzing me about where I was going.

I sent Ben a text to see if he wanted to come out and meet me somewhere, but got no reply, which was unusual.

I cycled all the way down to Manuka Park, just for something to do. It was deserted so I sat there on the kiddies' playground watching the sun rise slowly behind the trees of the reserve.

It was good. It was calm, and helped me focus my thinking on my big plans for the day. I had my bucket and twenty dollars borrowed from April's purse, now changed into small change, stashed in my backpack.

Roll on the Spring Fever School Fair.

I finally got there at about eleven. I wasn't sure if I was allowed to go, so I gave any teachers I saw a wide berth.

The first stall was just inside the school gate and run by Fizzer Boyd and his mates, Tupai, Jason, and Daniel the Warrior.

Tupai nodded at me as I sauntered casually past. 'Sorry to hear about the suspension,' he said.

I shrugged. 'What can you do?'

Tupai had his arms folded across his chest and looked quite tough, like a security guard or something. I suppose he was, in a way, because there was a fifty dollar note strung up at the front of their stall.

A sign on the stand announced, 'The Taste Test'. I wasn't sure what it was all about. I smiled politely at the other three guys, who all seemed to be genuinely concerned for me, and wandered on.

I passed the hot dog stand, and the huge white elephant stall. I was tempted to go and look through the bookstall but saw Miss Pepperman was helping run it, and I didn't want her to see me.

I eventually found myself down on bottom field where they were selling rides on quad bikes.

Ben was there with his parents. I had only met his mum and dad once or twice before and they had seemed pleasant enough, if a little over-protective.

They had grounded Ben after he had won that photo competition. Apparently, they had no idea he had been sneaking out to take photos of lightning, and all hell broke loose when they found out.

Ben looked startled when he saw me and dropped his eyes guiltily.

'Hi, mate,' I said.

'Hi,' he said heavily.

He wasn't worried about the chisel story, I realized, he had something else on his mind. He asked, 'Jacob, did you try to do that mind thing on me when you wanted me to run for the student council?'

'No,' I said honestly. 'I wouldn't do that to a mate.'

At that his mother looked around, then nudged his father.

'I didn't think so,' Ben said with a look of relief. Then his father stepped in front of him.

'You leave Ben alone from now on,' he said, stony-faced. 'Stay right away from him.'

I didn't have to be a genius to know why. News spreads quickly at Glenfield, and bad news spreads twice as fast as good. I was now Jacob the psychopathic chisel murderer, and good kids like Ben needed to be protected from evil fiends like me.

Ben's mother grabbed him by the arm and led him off through the throng. Ben looked back at me and mouthed, 'Sorry,' just before he disappeared. Ben's father followed them.

My breath was suddenly short. I wanted to hit somebody. I wanted to scream. Whatever I had done to Blocker, it didn't deserve this!

I realized I was crying and, without even thinking about where I was going, found myself on the covered walkway that led to the library.

The library. My refuge. My castle, ever since I was little.

There were footsteps across my path before I got there, though, and I looked up to see Erica with Stacey and Chelsie.

'Jacob!' she said with real concern in her voice. 'Are you all right?' She reached out to touch me but I blinked back the tears and pushed past her.

'Leave me alone,' I said with an overwhelming emptiness, and headed for the library. Safety.

The library was not part of the school fair and was deserted, which suited me fine. I was happiest alone. I didn't need Ben and I didn't need Erica.

Friends hurt you and it wasn't even their fault.

The library, on the other hand, was a place full of knowledge and excitement. You could learn about schoolboy spies in World War II or long lost underground civilisations.

I found something to read and sobbed quietly to myself while I waited for the end of the day.

For my crime time.

31

Crime Time

I left it until after four o'clock; after the fair had officially closed, and the procession of kids with their buckets or cash-tins of money had stopped flowing into the admin block. That was an important part of my ingenious plan. I wanted to be the last kid to arrive with a bucket of money and I wanted to arrive when they had already finished their counting.

My luck was in with the security guard at the entrance to the admin block. If it had been a teacher or Mr Curtis, then I would have been sunk because there was no way that a suspended kid was going to be bringing in a bucket of money.

But it wasn't, it was old Mrs Mandible, the parent-helper who ran the tuck-shop. But I had worked my magic on her once before so I was confident I could do it again.

It was time for phase one. Getting inside.

I pulled out my money-bucket, full of loose change, and tucked my backpack out of sight in the garden by the entrance to the hall. I casually entered the foyer. The entrance to the admin block was to the left, just past the school office.

Mandible sat on a wooden chair, reading. She looked up at me as I approached. 'Where's your pass?'

All the kids who would be carrying the fair proceeds needed a special pass to enter the admin block. Ben had shown me his.

'I dropped it somewhere,' I said with an apologetic shrug. 'But I showed it to you the last two times.'

I was counting on the fact that there would have been kids coming and going all day long bringing in the profits from the fair. She couldn't possibly remember them all. Plus she *had* seen my face before. And of course there was one more card to play.

That's right. I transmitted to her. *He was already in here a couple of times.*

She nodded, and waved me through. It was the end of the day, and one dropped pass was not going to cause any great problem.

I pushed open the heavy swing doors into the administration corridor. The last time I had been in here, it was to get kicked out of school by old Curtis. The door to his office was closed and no doubt locked, but I stuck my tongue out at it anyway. It didn't really make me feel any better though.

The next office was the Executive Officer's, then the small records room where they had set up the counting table.

The corridor was empty, which was as it should be. I glanced at the door at the far end of the corridor. After the crime, I would leave the money outside that door, then return the way I had come so as not to make Mandible suspicious. Then I would skirt around the outside of the hall and retrieve the money from where I had left it. Easy.

Except something was wrong.

The door at the end of the corridor was swinging open. It should have been locked. That didn't make any sense. Anybody could just walk in.

I wandered along the corridor and raised my hand to knock. I suppose I felt uneasy because it was only one day since I had left this corridor with my tail between my legs. Or, maybe, I was just uneasy about embarking on such an audacious crime. Whatever it was, it made me hesitate. And that saved my life.

As I paused, my glance fell back on the wide open door at the end of the corridor. And this time I noticed the really strange thing. The door was all splintered and broken around the lock. So was the door jamb.

The door hadn't been left unlocked, it had been forced open!

That stayed my hand a moment or two longer and, in that short space of time, the door to the room opened and a hideous creature began to back out into the corridor.

I froze for just a second, then, silently, began to creep backwards until my back touched the opposite wall.

The creature was the size of a man, dressed in a black rain-coat. Its back was bent over and hideously misshapen. A hunchback. It was carrying a large black rubbish bag and I knew at once what was in it. Money. The proceeds of the fair.

I knew also, without seeing, what the face would be. The horrible, distorted features of Quasimodo, the hunchback of Notre Dame.

I had come here to commit a robbery and I had walked in on one.

It was like a scene from a movie. There was an air of unreality about it. From outside, I could hear the shouts and laughter of excited children on their way home. From inside the hall behind me came the chatter of parent-helpers cleaning up after the big auction.

The Hunchback Robber eased himself out of the room, his attention on the two parent-helpers inside whose hands were bound with metallic tape. More tape covered their mouths. I'm not sure if they saw me or not. Their eyes were on the stubby shape of the sawn-off shotgun aimed directly at them.

It is hard to describe the emotions coursing through me at that moment. Fear? Of course. Terror even. Perhaps even a little excitement. The adrenalin was certainly flowing. Disbelief also. The Hunchback Robber had chosen the exact same day, and the exact same time, to rob exactly the same place I had planned to rob.

Of course, a part of my brain reasoned, while the rest screamed silently in terror, it was a tempting target, and if you were going to rob the takings of the fair, this was the logical time to do it: at the end of the day when the full proceeds were already in.

But the main emotion that flooded over me was one of indignation. This was my robbery. I had been planning this for weeks! What right did this thug have to walk in here with his shotgun and take over my crime?

But then I had another thought, and it was a doozie.

I could turn this around. Use it to my advantage. I would rob the robber!

It was the perfect crime. The Hunchback Robber would get all the blame, and I'd get all the money!

I thought quickly about how to pull it off. The main thing was not to get noticed.

Don't look around. Don't look around. I thought urgently at him.

The grotesque mask turned to the left, towards Curtis's office, then to the right, towards the open door. I was lucky, I

161

guess, the mask gave him a narrow field of vision and he could not see me, cowering against the wall right behind him.

It's all clear. It's all clear.

Satisfied, the hunchback pulled the door shut with a final menacing wave of his shotgun at the terrified occupants inside.

He immediately straightened and began walking towards the exit.

Just keep walking. Look straight ahead. I sent the message constantly. If he turned around, I was dead.

When he reached the door he checked carefully outside and, happy with what he saw, he dropped his bag to the floor.

With the ease of lots of practice he stripped off the raincoat, revealing, not a hump in his back, but just a very ordinary looking backpack strapped on to one shoulder.

The raincoat, the shotgun, and the bag of loot went quickly into the backpack and the Quasimodo mask followed. He stripped off thin rubber gloves and tossed them in as well. He was just an ordinary looking guy. He was facing away from me, but I could estimate his age. Late twenties or early thirties. Short hair. Nothing unusual, he looked like any non-descript guy carrying a backpack.

Just look straight ahead. Act natural. Don't seem guilty.

It was working. He picked up the bag without a backwards glance and stepped casually through the broken door. Strolling away from the building.

I followed a few paces behind. *Look straight ahead. Don't look back, that makes you look guilty.*

So that was how he vanished into thin air. He became a normal guy, and was immediately camouflaged in the people around him.

A moment or two later, we were walking out of the school grounds.

Don't look back.

32

Ill-gotten Gains

The old metal gates of the school swung out in a sudden gust of the approaching storm, moving as if to stop the thief. He turned left out of the gate and started to head up the hill towards the shopping mall. There were people everywhere. He was a part of the crowd.

We had gone less than a hundred metres, though, when the sound of sirens came from the top of the hill and two police cars came hurtling around the corner, lights flashing, sirens screaming, the whole deal. They stopped, parked on odd angles in the middle of the road, blockading the street.

Wow, that was fast.

The Hunchback Robber stopped in mid-stride, staring at the police cars. Two more had appeared and one of the road-blocks let them through. They raced down the hill towards us.

Hunchie made his mind up and turned around, heading straight for me. I wasn't worried, though. I, too, was just a part of the crowd.

I flicked a casual glance at his face as he passed by.

He had a thin goatee, but in all other respects was a very ordinary-looking guy.

He headed down the hill now. I knew exactly what to do and poured thought after thought at him.

It's too risky now. Stash the backpack and come back for it later when the coast is clear.

He crossed the road, moving towards the bush reserve in the gully at the bottom of the hill.

I stayed on the other side of the road. In the crowd.

He disappeared into the bush and I waited. I knew he would emerge sooner or later, you couldn't go anywhere that way, it just led to a wide deep creek. A second or two later he re-appeared, minus the backpack, in time to see two more police cars screech to a halt around the corner at the bottom of the road and set up a road-block there.

There was enormous confusion in the crowd. What was going on? I could almost hear them wondering.

Hunchie crossed back over and blended right in. Just another face in the crowd.

He headed back into the school grounds, and why shouldn't he? Without any witnesses to identify him, without any incriminating loot, he was just one of the fair-goers.

I waited until he was safely out of sight and strolled across the road, as natural as anything. Without being obvious about it, I stepped slowly into the bush.

There was only one way in, a kind of a track beaten by kids from the college. The bush surrounded me and smothered the noise too, except for the wailing sirens. Then they too switched off, and the silence was enveloping.

Where would he hide it?

The rain began. I pulled up my collar and moved deeper into the bush. In the distance I heard thunder. The gloom intensified as the rain increased.

Where would he hide it?

I searched behind tree trunks and in the centre of dense bushes. Nothing.

I beat my way through the thicker bushes to the left, then to the right of the small path. Nothing. Yet it had to be here.

Lightning flashed in the distance, filtered though the leaves, and I looked up involuntarily. That was how I found it. A glimpse of yellow and red, high above the ground in the fork of an old kowhai.

It was out of my reach, but that was not going to stop me now. I threw myself at the tree, scrabbling madly at the trunk and, somehow, got the tips of my fingers to the edge of a strap. I tugged, and the bag came loose, tumbling on to my head with a thump that I barely noticed.

With trembling hands I unzipped it and pulled open the black plastic bag inside.

It was exactly the way I had imagined. Piles and piles of notes of every description. Edmund Hillary and Kate Sheppard and even a few Lord Rutherfords. Untold wealth.

And it was all mine.

I closed the bag and put it on my back. I couldn't leave it here. It was a bit risky taking it out, with all the cops everywhere, but, I reasoned, they were looking for an adult hunchback, not a kid with a backpack.

Lightning flashed again and thunder roared, closer this time. I was starting to get drenched.

I emerged from the relative peace of the bush to the whirlwind confusion of the road. The rain was washing the steep street; people were scurrying up and down the hill. The red and blue lights of the police cars swept wetly around the scene from both ends of the road.

I started to walk and, abruptly, stopped. There she was. Directly opposite me. Erica. The most wonderful creature in all creation.

What would she think? my mind kept asking over and over. What would she think of me if she knew I really was a bad egg? A trouble-maker. A criminal. A thief.

I froze, with one foot in the air, overwhelmed by it all. This was it. I could walk off with the loot and be rich. There was a line that I was about to cross, like the line in the canteen, but this one would decide what kind of person I would grow up to be.

My foot came down. All I had to do was to walk up the hill, away from the school. Away from the police. Away from Erica.

I looked at Erica and she turned around and looked me square in the eyes. To this day, I don't know if I did that with my power, made her look at me, I mean. Maybe it was just coincidence.

But she looked at me and I looked at her, and that moment was worth all the loot in the world. That instant in time was the end of my criminal career.

I took a step in the other direction, towards the police. There was a crowd of them, milling around, looking harassed and urgent.

I walked up to the nearest policeman and thrust the bag towards him.

'Not now, son,' he said.

'No, no,' I began. 'I followed him, and . . .'

'Please move away and let us do our work.' He turned away abruptly at a call from another officer.

I walked up to him and tapped him on the arm but, before

167

I could get a word in, he thrust an angry finger at my face. 'Go, move away, get out of here! Now!'

'But I . . .'

'Go!'

He turned away again.

'But I followed the robber and found his bag!' I screamed, tearing open the zipper on the bag to show him.

He half turned. They all did, watching in slow motion as the mask and coat fell out, followed by the shotgun, which hit the ground muzzle first and fired.

I don't know much about guns, and especially not shotguns, I thought they had safety catches, but either this one didn't or it was off.

The explosion was like a bomb bursting and, if the gun had been facing upwards, it might have been a disaster. The flash of the shot illuminated all the blue uniforms and the crash of the shot was like a shockwave through the crowd.

They gasped and cowered in an instant as the shotgun took off like a rocket, kicking into the air with the force of the blast. It shot up about ten metres, seemed to hover there for a few seconds, then slowly started to fall, right into the astonished arms of a police constable.

There was a shocked silence for a few seconds, our ears all ringing with the noise of the shot. Then the police reacted. I looked up at a sea of blue uniforms, and some of them had guns. And those guns were pointing at me.

33

The Getaway

'Drop the bag and put your hands behind your head,' a voice barked.

'I found it!' I shouted again, trying not to show the stark cold terror that I felt. There were guns pointed at me.

'That's Jacob Smith,' I heard someone call out. 'He goes to our school.'

That wasn't quite true, after the session with Mr Curtis, but it was close enough for me.

The cops seemed to relax a bit at that, but the guns did not waver. 'Drop the bag and put your hands behind your head.'

I dropped the bag. I put my hands behind my head and clasped them together to stop them shaking.

'Now lie down!'

The grass was soaking wet! Still, I wasn't about to argue with an armed bunch of cops. I lay down beside the bag and called out desperately, 'I followed the robber! He stashed the bag in the bush, but I found it! I saved the school!'

As I did so I aimed a single thought at all the policemen I could see. Lightning flashed again and lit up their faces and I lit up their minds with two small words.

It's true.

They believed me. Suddenly, I was just a small frightened boy lying on a muddy bank. More than that. A hero. Guns vanished. Policemen were all around me, strong hands helping me to my feet, brushing mud from my clothes. A police tunic was draped around my shoulders, some relief from the pouring rain.

Police surrounded me, and a crowd of onlookers surrounded them, a multi-coloured sea of umbrellas and rain-coats completely blocking the road.

I gabbled out what had happened. Well, as much of it as I could and still appear to be a hero and not a villain.

'I saw him in the admin block,' I said, 'and followed him. It was the Hunchback Robber! I couldn't let him get away.'

A policewoman in plain clothes poured me a cup of coffee out of a thermos and, as she did so, I looked up at the crowd of onlookers. I saw Ben, and his parents. Blocker was there, and Miss Pepperman. There was Jenny Kreisler, looking wet, cold and alarmed, clutching the arm of Phil Domane. And Erica. Standing next to . . . Oh my God!

There he was. The cheeky son-of-a-bum. Right in the middle of the crowd. The invisible man. The man who could disappear into thin air. The Hunchback Robber. And he didn't look happy.

'That's him!' I yelled, dropping the hot coffee all over my shoes and pointing. 'That's him!'

The crowd's eyes turned towards the man, who, after an initial startled glance, broke suddenly and ran. The police were all around me, there were none close enough to stop him. He headed for the school grounds, where he could lose himself amongst all the buildings.

The crowd parted like the red sea, recoiling from the wild eyes and frantic windmilling limbs. And then there was only one kid in front of him. One kid between the running man and freedom.

What a shame, for the Hunchback Robber I mean, that it was Tupai White.

34

Finger Prints

The policewoman was nice. Her name was Minet Brits, Detective Constable Minet Brits. She had kind eyes, although you could see the toughness that was there as well. You had to be pretty tough to be a police officer, I guess. She had poured me another cup of coffee and this one stayed in the cup and it felt good.

I was a hero.

Mandible had seen the whole thing. Apparently she had entered the corridor just in time to see me cowering against the wall.

Very brave, I was, according to her, the way I set out after the robber without a thought for my own safety. Mandible had seen the shotgun and, wisely, kept her mouth shut. She had quietly gone for the phone instead, which explained why the cops were there so quickly.

If I had looked behind me, I would have seen her, but I was too busy making sure that the robber didn't look behind him, to think of looking behind me!

In all the excitement and confusion no-one thought to ask why I was in the corridor in the first place, which was lucky.

I was sitting, holding my coffee, with a warm towel around my soaked and muddy shoulders, on the leather sofa in Mr Curtis's office. The same leather sofa my parents had been sitting on the day before.

Curtis didn't know what to make of the whole affair.

He sat silently behind his desk while we waited for my parents, and stared out through the open door at the finger-print guys dusting fine white powder over the door frames.

Eventually he said, 'I'm sorry Jacob, but this doesn't change a thing.'

I hadn't really thought it would.

DC Brits sat next to me on the sofa.

'Can I get you anything else?' she asked. 'Are you hungry?'

I wasn't really, but I knew never to turn down free food, so I nodded.

A constable was sent up the road, and, while we were waiting, DC Brits said, 'What you did was foolish, and stupid, you know that don't you?'

'I guess.'

'He had a shotgun. You might have been killed.'

'I know,' I smiled. 'I promise not to do it again.'

She smiled back. 'But we're not going to make a big deal about that side of things to your parents, OK. You are a hero, and that's all they need to know. Your mum would have a fit if she knew what the dangers really were.'

'That's fine by me,' I said.

She put her arm around me and gave my shoulders a squeeze.

'And you were a hero today. You really were. Your name will be put forward for a bravery medal. And if there is ever anything we can do for you, you just need to ask.'

'Really?' I said slowly, an idea starting to dawn.

'Well, almost anything.'

I looked outside at the fingerprint guys in their clean white overalls and then at the chisel, still sitting on Curtis's desk where Saltham had put it the previous day.

'There is one thing,' I said.

Mum, Dad and a cheeseburger all arrived simultaneously and, although I had thought I wasn't hungry, the food disappeared in seconds. Mum and Dad turned up in Mrs McLatcheon's Morris Minor with Gumbo sitting in the back seat. It took another twenty minutes of explanations and a lot of fussing and 'crikeys' from Mum before my parents were anywhere near satisfied they understood what had happened.

The first camera crew turned up five minutes after that. They were from TV3 and they beat the TV1 news crew by almost sixty seconds. The *Crime Time* team were much slower. The other reporters had already got their shots and done their interviews by the time *Crime Time* got there.

I'd turned into something of a celebrity. The boy who'd caught the Hunchback Robber. Well, I suppose technically that was Tupai, but it was me they wanted to talk to.

I gave the same interview, almost word for word, to both TV crews and when I finally got to meet the *Crime Time* producer I was exhausted.

His name was Nicholas Priddey.

'How are you feeling, Jacob?' he asked.

'A little tired,' I said honestly. 'Where's PC Plod?'

He looked startled at first and then laughed. 'Is that what you call him?'

'Sorry, I didn't mean . . .'

'No, no,' he laughed again. 'That's the nickname we use as well, when he's not around. But don't tell anybody I told you.'

I laughed with him. 'Promise.'

Priddey said, 'He doesn't come out on shoots. He just records linking pieces in the studio afterwards.'

Dad came over, holding Gumbo on a short leash, and stood next to me while the *Crime Time* team fitted me up with a lapel microphone attached to a small black box on my waist.

'We're almost ready to go,' Priddey said. 'Our interview will be a little longer than the news crews do. They just want short sound bites, but we want the whole story.'

He turned to Dad. 'We'll interview you next, detective, just get you to say what a hero Jacob is, that sort of thing.'

Dad shook his head. 'I'm not a detective.'

'He's my dad,' I clarified.

Priddey looked confused. 'I'm sorry. We've met before haven't we? I was sure you were with the police.'

Dad said, 'I'm an actor. I had a role on your show a few weeks ago.'

But I burst out laughing because I knew why Priddey was so confused.

I said, 'He's the policeman from the dog-food commercial!'

The interview took about five minutes, and, by the time we had finished, one of the fingerprint guys had lifted three sets of prints off the chisel.

Not surprisingly, one set proved to be Dad's. Curtis had asked Old Sea Salt to come in. He stood rubbing the ink off his fingertips with a tissue while they confirmed another set were his.

The third set of prints weren't mine.

'Well, whose are they then?' asked Curtis.

Jeez he could be thick sometimes. How did he ever get put in charge of a school?

'Get Blocker, I mean Markus, in here,' I suggested.

Saltham said, 'I saw him a few moments ago. I'll go and find him.'

I watched Curtis's face carefully while we waited. He seemed afraid to look at me. He had been wrong about me. Not only was I now a hero of the school, but it turned out that I might have been telling the truth yesterday as well!

Saltham arrived back with not only Blocker in tow, but his mother as well.

Gumbo saw them coming in the door and started to growl. Dad had to haul back on the leash to restrain him.

'What is going on?' Frau Blüchner demanded.

Mr Curtis said simply, 'The police have fingerprinted the chisel. Jacob's prints are not on it. We'd like to get a sample of Markus's prints so we can exclude him as well.'

Frau Blüchner looked at Blocker, who looked horrified.

'Well?' Mr Curtis asked Blocker.

'No!' he blurted out at last. 'You can't make me!'

'Can we?' Curtis asked DC Brits curtly.

She shook her head. 'He's a minor and he hasn't been arrested for anything. He has to volunteer to give his prints.'

I couldn't help myself, I said, 'So, volunteer, Blocker.'

'No!' he blurted. 'I'm not going to.'

Dad tried to calm things down. 'Listen, son, if they're not your prints then . . .'

But the older Blüchner thundered in as lightning flashed outside.

'If Markus said he didn't do it, then he didn't do it! You do not have to treat him like a criminal.'

The problem was, by now it was pretty obvious to everyone in the room that Markus *was* a criminal. The guilty expression on his face left little room for doubt.

Frau Blüchner started to say something else, but Saltham cut her off. 'Jacob, I'd like you and your parents to wait outside for a few moments while we discuss this. You too, Markus.'

Curtis looked panic stricken and I wasn't surprised. The thought of being shut in a room with those two going head to head would have been terrifying.

Detective Constable Brits came with us and pulled the door shut.

To my surprise, Ben was there.

'Ben!' I exclaimed. 'Where are your mum and dad?' I looked around nervously for them.

He shrugged with a 'who cares?' attitude. 'Probably out looking for me.'

'Hi, Jacob,' came a voice from behind me. I whirled around to see Erica sitting on the other side of the corridor.

'Erica.' I dropped my eyes to the floor. I couldn't believe how I had treated her outside the library.

She stood and hugged me tightly, never mind who was watching.

'I'm sorry,' I mumbled, but she shushed me.

'No need to be,' she said.

We heard most of what went on in Curtis's office through the thin wooden door but I won't repeat it here.

All I will tell you is that in the space of ten minutes in that confined space, a Panzer Tank took on a Navy Destroyer, and lost. I sat on the seat between Ben and Erica, and thought that, just maybe, things were going to be OK.

Mum said nothing, but there was a smile on her face every time she looked at me. Or was it *Erica and me* she was looking at? Mums can be a bit funny about girlfriends.

Dad spent the time trying to get Gumbo to stop growling at Blocker.

Frau Blüchner burst out of the office a few moments later, white of face and wide of eye. She grabbed Blocker by the arm. He was in for it when they got home, anyone could see that.

Mr Curtis came to the door of his office. He looked a bit ashen, but he was coping well.

He motioned to Mum and Dad. 'Can I see you for a moment?'

Dad passed Gumbo's lead to me and went into Curtis's office with Mum.

Through the doors I could see Frau Blüchner dragging Blocker off though the carpark, unmindful of the weather. Her piercing voice cut through the rain back to us, inside.

Without warning Blocker wrenched his arm out of his mother's grip and ran off into the thundering storm.

That was too much for Gumbo, who had been sitting there restraining himself for too long. He jumped up, jerking the lead from my hand and went haring outside after Blocker.

'Gumbo!' I yelled, but it did no good. I cursed to myself and ran out after him.

35

The Pylon

Gumbo ran, and I ran, and Ben ran with me, and, somewhere in front of us all, was Blocker.

Rain pelted us and lightning lit the rapidly approaching night. Without raincoats we were soaked in seconds. It was freezing and miserable. Rain ran down the back of our necks and lashed at our eyes.

I don't know where Blocker was going, but it wasn't home. He took off up the side street, towards Manuka Ridge. I glanced behind and Ben was right there, and Erica too.

Gumbo was surprisingly quick for an old dog but his legs could not hold out and, eventually, he stopped and looked back waiting for us to catch up.

I peered through the rain up the hill where I could see a brief flash of Blocker's jumper.

'Where's he going?' I shouted, holding on to Gumbo's collar, but I already knew.

Thanks to Ben's prize-winning photo, there wasn't a kid in school who didn't know about the power pylon on Manuka Ridge and the way it attracted lightning.

'The pylon!' Ben confirmed my thoughts. Lightning cracked

its way across the sky nearby, followed soon after by rolling thunder.

'Go after him,' Erica yelled, her hair in her eyes.

I hesitated.

'Go after him,' she repeated. 'You can't just leave him!'

She grabbed Gumbo's collar out of my hand and said, 'I'll bring your dog.'

We ran. The wind was freezing my legs and my lungs were beginning to gasp for air. Beside me, Ben ran effortlessly, mechanically, tirelessly, robotically.

By the time we got to the top of Manuka Ridge my chest was burning and my guts were retching. Blocker had turned into Ridge Road, towards the pylon.

Something about that scared me in a way I hadn't been scared before and my legs found new strength.

Lightning cracked again, and thunder drummed all around us only a few seconds later.

'Three seconds!' Ben shouted into my ear. 'Just three kilometres away!'

The pylon stood, sentry like, in its empty grassy field. Up this close, I could see that the legs were set into huge concrete blocks. It soared into the sky above us, impossibly tall when viewed from its base.

About six metres up the pylon, completely encircling it, was a horizontal fence of barbed wire, jutting sideways out from the structure to prevent anyone climbing it.

Blocker was clinging to the tower, a dark figure, just below the barbs of the barrier.

Lighting flared again. 'Two seconds!' Ben shouted.

We ran up close to the base of the pylon and I had to gasp some air back into my lungs.

'Come down!' I shouted into the driving rain. 'You'll be killed!'

Blocker said nothing. He was gripping the strut of the pylon with grim determination against the gusting wind.

Beside me, Ben said, 'I think that's the idea.'

'Blocker!' I screamed.

He turned away from us and put his elbow around a strut for better support.

Without stopping to think, I ran forward and started to climb. The struts were icy cold and slippery. My foot slipped twice, crashing my knee into a sharp metal edge, and I clung on desperately before regaining my footing.

I was a couple of metres high when there was a different voice. A female voice, terrified.

'Jacob, get down!' It was Erica.

I ignored her and kept climbing. Lightning flashed and, almost immediately, the thunder followed. For a second, I froze with fear, then realized we hadn't been struck. It would have already been all over if we had.

'One second!' Ben yelled. 'It's right on top of us!'

I hauled myself up to Blocker's level and shouted at him. He turned to face me. He was bawling his eyes out.

'It's not worth it!' I screamed. 'Not this!'

He shook his head, and shouted back over the noise of the wind and rain. 'You have no idea. You don't know what it's like. Since Dad died . . .' and that was all he could say.

Amidst it all I reflected, once again, how you never really know what is going on inside people.

'It's not worth it,' I repeated, but it had no effect. I tried to focus my power on him but I already knew it wouldn't work; it never did against fierce determination. 'Blocker,' I said, moving closer so that I wouldn't have to shout. 'I don't know what your life is like. How could I? I'm not you. But the way I see it, life is like a book. There are good chapters and bad chapters. But when you get to a bad chapter, you don't stop reading the book!'

He looked up at me and it seemed something was getting through.

I continued, 'If you do, then you never get to find out what happens next!'

He looked hesitant now. I couldn't remember how long it had been since the last lightning flash.

I bellowed, 'You've only just started the book.'

He unhooked his elbow from the strut but still gripped the grey metal tightly.

'You've gotta want to find out what happens next!' I repeated, and his grip loosened.

'Get outa there!' Ben's voice screamed from below.

'Let go, Blocker!' I cried and hit him with the full force of my power at the same time.

Let go! Let go! Let go! Let go! Let go! Let go!

His hands straightened and his grip failed. He dropped the few metres to the ground below.

I glanced down to see Erica helping him away from the base of the pylon. To safety. I looked up at the rumbling black clouds above and breathed a long slow sigh of relief.

'Jacob!' Ben yelled and my brain started working properly again. Blocker was safe, but *I was still clinging to the tower*.

I leaped away from the pylon just as a blinding flash enveloped me. My nostrils were filled with the smell of ozone and my eardrums burst with the explosions of ten nuclear bombs all going off simultaneously.

But I was in the air and falling and, somehow, I sensed Ben running forwards below me.

I landed in his arms, but it was too much weight and all he really did was break my fall. I thought I heard a sharp crack, but it was difficult to be sure with my ears ringing with the thunder.

I rolled off Ben. The grass was hot. Wet, but burning hot. I rolled and rolled, away from the heat, away from the danger.

There was a warm, wet sensation on my face, and it took me a moment to realize it was Gumbo, slopping and slobbering all over me.

'I'm all right, Gumbo, I'm all right,' I said, and looked around for Ben. He was a few metres away and obviously in a lot of pain. His arm was broken. The skin was torn and a jagged white edge of a bone poked out through it.

He had done that trying to break my fall.

Ben Holly. My mate.

'Ben!' I said, in that weird dream-like world of shock where crazy things make perfect sense. 'Ben, you're not a robot after all.'

And Ben, despite the pain, began to laugh.

36

The Big Game

The next weekend, for reasons I didn't fully understand, I invited Blocker around to watch the grand final of the NRL with Ben and me.

His mother didn't think it was such a great idea, but his counsellor thought it would do him some good. So Blocker was with us when we watched Daniel score the winning try, with just seconds to go, against the Warrior's old foes: The Blacktown Machetes.

The three of us leapt to our feet screaming as he dived over the line, lost the ball, recovered it, and slammed it down for the try.

Gumbo went wild, running round and round in tight circles and knocking over Mum's precious antique clock on the side table, which we didn't even notice until the next day.

Mrs Blüchner came around in a big old BMW to pick Blocker up after the game. He was on very tight reigns.

And, while we were waiting for his mother, Blocker told me about the lightning tower.

'I really couldn't hear anything you were saying,' he said slowly, staring at the floor. 'But, after all the crap I put you through, you still climbed the tower and risked your life to save me. I couldn't understand why you'd do that.'

He lifted his gaze, looked me dead in the eye and said, 'That was why I let go.'

On the Monday following, Dad got offered a job. It turned out that, for some time, *Crime Time* had been looking for a new presenter. PC Plod just wasn't up to it. Dad wasn't a cop, but he looked like one. One thing led to another, and he got invited to audition.

He won the role. Long-term. On-going. Well paid. We celebrated with a dinner out in a real flash restaurant.

I had known all along he would get the job, though. There was never any doubt in my mind.

I had been sitting next to the producer at the audition.

37

Epilogue

Gumbo died the other day. But I don't want you to feel sad about it. He was old. He'd had a long life and a good one. It's OK for me to feel sad, he was my dog. I'd known him my entire life. My lovable, big, old floppy, sloppy dog. But I don't want you to feel bad.

Two years have now passed, almost to the day, since that frightening night on the power pylon and many other things have changed as well.

Erica and I went out together for more than a year before we decided to break it off. I think she's quite keen on Tupai White nowadays but Erica, being Erica, is too shy to say anything. I think he might like her too, but I'm not sure.

Ben and I are still real good mates, and a few months ago I persuaded him to run for the Youth Parliament. That's when teenagers are invited to run a mock Government for a few days during Parliamentary recess. It was like the student council thing all over again. He got in, and I wasn't at all surprised when he got elected the Youth Prime Minister.

I ran into Markus Blüchner the other day. His mother took him out of Glenfield and sent him to an expensive private school after the whole affair. He said hello quite warmly, if with a certain amount of embarrassment. He wasn't the same kid I had lived in fear of for so long. He seemed to have learned you don't have to intimidate people to get them to like you.

As for my special power, well I'm taking that under advisement. I've kind of gone off the whole super-villain idea. Maybe I'll become a super-hero. Who knows? Or maybe, like Old Sea Salt, I'll decide to do nothing with my power at all. I have plenty of time to decide. I'm still a teenager.

One thing I am more and more sure of though is this: life really is like a book, and when I'm old and wrinkly and creaking away in a wooden rocking chair on the porch of some old-folks' home, reminiscing about my life, I want to have written a book I'm proud of, not one I'm ashamed of.

But whatever I do, I'll need a new nickname.

Nobody calls me Freak any more.

38

Appendix:
Wise and Wonderful Words

Agenda
What grown-ups do when they have meetings because otherwise they'd forget what they're talking about and just argue about silly stuff the whole time. It's a list of the topics to discuss in the meeting.

Advisement
Under advisement is just a fancy way of saying that you will go and get advice from others on this. Business people talk in language like this all the time.

Anonymous
When nobody knows who is responsible.

Arduous
Something that is difficult to achieve, like the top level on Halo 2.

Brusquely
Look it up in the dictionary. It'll be good practice.

Circumspect
This means to be cautious, but it's a bit stronger than that, it's like you've taken every possibility into account before doing anything.

Clinical
This is the best word I could think of to describe my great mate Ben. I used it in the sense of precise, exact and unemotional.

Conspicuously
The word means clearly visible or attracting notice.

Derision
Another word would be ridicule.

Disembowel
To have all your innards and guts and stuff ripped out, like in those cool stories about knights and ancient warriors.

Emphatically
To use great emphasis in the way you speak, or move, or the words you say.

Enormity
Enormity has lots of meanings. I used it to mean something that was totally outrageous.

Ensconce
For example, to tuck away somewhere, nice and safe and snug.

Excruciation
Great torment, or in other words, not a lot of fun!

Futile
Totally useless. Like my sister April.

Humility

The dictionary says humbleness. I used this word to show that Ben did not seek fame or fortune for doing something that he thought was simply the right thing to do.

Impervious

Sort of tough, and not affected by stuff around it. I wish I was impervious.

Inconceivable

Something so far beyond reason and understanding, that your mind cannot even grasp it. Like the infinite size of the universe. Or the size of an atom.

Indomitable

What a great word. Strong, unyielding, stubbornly persistent. I wish I was that, too.

Malevolent

This is a wonderful word to say out loud, just feel the way your mouth moves when you say it, mal-ev-o-lent. It means really, really evil, and wanting to do bad stuff.

Malignant

Why are all the evil words so much fun to say? Mal-ig-nant. Try it. Slowly. If you're talking about a disease it means something that spreads quickly or is infectious. But I used it to mean nasty, or harmful.

Minutiae

All the fine details, ins and outs, ups and downs, etc.

Noisome

I used this word deliberately, knowing that Blocker wouldn't understand what it meant. It means harmful, noxious, evil-smelling, objectionable or offensive. Use this word as often as you can!

Pedantic

Just to be a little fuss-pot about stuff and insist on everything being perfect. You know people like that. Teachers mainly.

Persecution

To ill-treat. I guess Old Sea Salt didn't really persecute kids, but it felt like it to me sometimes.

Perversely

Different from what is reasonable. I really mean that I liked Frau Blüchner as a teacher, when nobody in their right minds would. But I already explained my reasons for that.

Profile

When you're talking about actors, their profile is their livelihood. It means how well known they are. Wearing a mask did not help Dad's profile one bit. Even the producer of the show hardly recognised him later!

Succinct

Pronounce this one as suck-sinked. Short and to the point.

Testament

When someone said good stuff about you it was a *testament* to you that . . .

Tirade

Fancy word for someone going on and on at you about stuff.

Uncommonly

Means *remarkably*. Just a different way of saying it so it doesn't get boring.

Viable

Spanish word for the devil. No just kidding, that's *Diablo*. Viable means do-able. It's kind of the opposite of impossible.